I0738726

AIR SERIES ⬥ BOOK 5

FENRISÚLFR

NOVELLA

AMANDA BOOLOODIAN

License Notes

Printed in the United States of America

Copyright © 2017 Amanda Booloodian
Published by: Walton INK

Cover Art by Deranged Doctor Design
Formatting by Michael Booloodian

ISBN-13:978-0-9973353-9-2

Walton INK
booloodian.com

DEDICATION

Dedicated to my parents. Thank you for everything.

CONTENTS

Mandatory leave. That's what I was faced with. There were no appeals available, and arguing would only make me look bad during all the psych evaluations that I had to look forward to.

The agency might as well have posted a sign telling me I screwed up my job.

Gran was safe, though, and completely unfazed by the fact that someone had threatened her to get to me. After firing her gun in the house, she had ringing in her ears, but beyond that, she was unharmed, which left me relieved. Rider was on the mend, but wasn't interested in speaking with me or letting me know what had gone wrong between us.

My response? It was a perfect time to take a vacation. It might have looked like I was running away, but that's because I was.

After I had arranged for Susan to take Gran to her upcoming doctor's appointment, I packed my bags and left town. Even better, my boyfriend, Ethan, was able to join me.

Originally, I intended to sit on a beach for a week and get

up only when the drinks were empty, but Ethan had other ideas in mind. When we got to our secluded mountain cabin, with no Wi-Fi, spotty phone service, and no other living person for miles around, I knew he was right. This was the perfect place.

"Cassie, wake up," Ethan whispered.

"I'm awake," I mumbled into my pillow while I kept my eyes shut.

In truth, I was up the moment he moved. Having someone to share my bed with wasn't something I was used to. Still, I was in adamant denial of the fact that I was awake well before dawn while on vacation.

"We're going to miss the sunrise," Ethan said.

"Humph." Watching the sunrise had sounded like a good idea when we found the ridge on yesterday's hike. In the dark hours of the morning, however, while lying comfortable in the bed and my boyfriend only an arm's length away, it wasn't on the top of my list of things to do.

Ethan chuckled, laid back down beside me, and then put his arm around me. He was already dressed. Number two on my list of things to do was out, and number one, sleep, was being driven out of the building as well.

"The starry night out there won't last long," Ethan said, "but it's a beautiful view in here. We could stay in."

A grin broke out across my face as I blushed and then opened my eyes. "You're right, it's a good view." So far, it had been two amazing days and nights with Ethan. Yesterday, we even managed to go on a short hike. Today, however, we told ourselves that we would go out into the world for the whole day.

Looking into Ethan's eyes in the dim light, I gave him a long kiss.

"So," he said, sliding closer to me, "we're staying in this morning?"

Laughing, I pushed myself slightly away. "No, this morning we see the stars."

He closed the distance between us and kissed me. It didn't last as long this time. "It's difficult to think of leaving the house with you here next to me."

"I guess that means I had better get dressed." I stretched out beside him, getting ready to leave the bed in search of clothes.

"Mmm." Ethan ran his hand down the line of my body.

Before I had finished stretching, he leaned up on his elbow and was over me, kissing me.

I giggled through the kiss and folded my arms around him, bringing him closer.

The sun was well over the horizon before we made it out of the cabin.

THE DRIVE to town took more than an hour, one of the pitfalls of being in the middle of nowhere. Only a few months into our relationship, we used the time to talk without the distractions we'd succumbed to at the cabin.

Tomorrow morning, dark and early, we would try again for sunset on the ridge.

As we approached town, I watched trees emerged from the forest and vanish into it again as they passed by the window. "I really needed this."

Ethan was quiet for a while, but then reached out and took my hand. "Do you want to talk about it?"

"About what?" I asked.

Ethan gripped my hand. "Darling, you were taken from your home by a man that wanted to kill you."

I didn't look away from the window, but I didn't see the trees anymore. "Einar didn't do anything to me."

"But Rider-"

I tensed at the words. "Is okay. He's back on his feet."

"It's great that he bounced back so quickly." Ethan was forcing his words to sound lighter. "I still can't believe that one of your partners is a werewolf."

A partner that was supposed to be a friend, but wouldn't talk to me. By werewolf custom, friendship should be an unbreakable bond between us, but I could see the cracks starting to form between me and Rider.

"So, are there any mythological creatures in these parts?" Ethan asked.

I could tell he was trying to salvage the conversation, so I decided to put on a smile. "Any Lost, you mean? I didn't think to check the records." The agency I worked for, the Agency for Interdimensional Regulation, worked with people and creatures from other dimensions that were trapped in this world, or that had moved here intentionally. "I imagine with all the woods, there are several in the area, though."

"What type would live out here?" Ethan sounded genuinely curious, so I looked away from the window and away from the ugly memories of my last few cases.

I thought over his question. "The area is large enough to hide pretty much anything. Fairies, gnomes, and pixies, can take up a relatively small area, even with the whole family living together. Out here, though, a herd of centaur could go unnoticed. A large tribe of goblins would be right at home as well. Any of the larger, more solitary people could hide and never be seen."

"Larger?"

I looked over at Ethan and he looked like his head was spinning. He was also taking a lot more glances into the woods beside the road.

"Elves can fit in pretty much anywhere," I said. "But a big troll or ogre can't go to town anytime they want. Well, it's discouraged anyway."

"It's hard to imagine that all of those different creatures are here," Ethan said.

"People," I corrected.

"What?"

"People. Everyone I mentioned is a person. Creature implies they're animals. We have those as well, but anyone who's intelligent is a person."

"Sorry."

"Want to have lunch after we get supplies?" I asked, trying to change the subject.

Ethan shifted in his seat. "Uh, yeah, we can do that. It's a long ride back, so we'll want to pick up any perishables after lunch."

He looked uncomfortable, but it wasn't until we settled into a booth at a local diner a few hours later that I realized why.

Despite putting on my best smile, the waitress pretty much ignored me. Months ago my soul had been torn to shreds. After that day, it was almost impossible to make a good first impression. Some people instantly hated me, while others ignored my existence, even Ethan. He had been practically hostile towards me when we first met.

Rider described it as 'natural selection in action.' The damage to my soul could be felt by those around me, so they reacted in unexpected ways. Most people were too wrapped up in themselves, so they didn't notice. The smartest people I had met stared, as if I was some sort of puzzle they had to figure out.

If someone felt unsure or uncomfortable with themselves, they tended to ignore me, or they purposefully tried to wreak havoc on my day. It was the people that were dominant, natural predators, or just cranky and looking for a reason to lash out that I had the most problems with. They were more prone to get physical.

Once people had been around me for a while, they got over it. No matter how nice I acted, though, there was no way the waitress was going to treat me with anything but contempt.

When I didn't get my drink, I excused myself and let Ethan do my ordering. Since I didn't particularly want to get back to the table before the food arrived, I turned on my phone to check for a signal.

Two whole bars. I guess we're back to civilization.

I waved the phone at Ethan and motioned that I was going to step outside. Standing in the warm, early summer sun, I called Gran.

"Mornin', sugar," Gran said when she picked up the phone.

I forgot about the time difference. Gran was an hour behind me, so it was still before noon there. "Morning. I wanted to call to see how things are going."

"That mother of yours is plumb crazy. She's been over here twice this week fussin' about the plants I threw out while I was stayin' there."

"Mom's been there twice in only a few days? That doesn't sound like her."

"It has to be more than those fake things I threw out. There were so many that I'm surprised she even noticed some were gone."

I bit my lip. "Did she say anything about her trip with Bob?"

"Not a thing. If she fusses about the plants again, I'm going to introduce her to CiCi, or your rabbit."

"Don't show her Frank. I'll never hear the end of it." The idea of my mother knowing about my zombie bunny made my anxiety climb to new levels.

"Maybe seeing CiCi living in the backyard will work. It would mess with her safe and normal world too much if she knew we had a fairy."

"Maybe."

"Still, it's nice to see her around once she's done talkin' about her plants, especially without that husband of hers. How is your trip?"

"It's nice. We're having a good time."

"Well, don't let anyone ruin your fun," Gran said.

"Is anything likely to?"

"You're so far away that it's hard to say for sure. I get the feeling somethin's going to get in your way, but don't let it, and have fun with your detective."

"Thanks, Gran."

"Dee Dee is gonna be here soon."

"I'll let you go, but my cell phone will be off again later today. There's no signal out here."

"Take care and enjoy every second with your fella."

"Thanks, Gran."

Looking inside, I could see the food was arriving at our table, so I went back in. Since I had called Gran, the phone made a connection to the outside world, and now that world was intruding. Messages were pouring in on my phone.

"How's your grandmother?" Ethan asked.

Ethan already knew me so well. "She's doing okay. It sounds like Mom is driving her nuts."

"They don't get along?"

"Not when Mom is with her husband, or when Mom is complaining about something."

"How about you, do you get along with your mother?" Ethan asked.

"She wants me to get a job where she works." I tried not to scrunch up my face in disgust.

He chuckled. "I'm guessing not as an agent?"

"As an accountant."

"Is she a, um, Reader, like you?"

Glancing around, I saw no one close enough to overhear unless they were really trying. Still, I dropped my voice. "I'm the only Reader in the family. Gran and Mom are psychic." Being a Reader is why I have the job that I do. I'm not a stellar agent, but my ability to see what people have been doing, reading the atmosphere of a place, and if necessary, using my power to calm down tense situations, makes me a valuable team member. It's usually people reacting to my soul that causes the need to smooth over incidents, but it's useful all the same.

"Is that normal?"

A burst of laughter tumbled out of me. "Is there any part of that sentence that's normal?"

Ethan chuckled, then reached out and took my hand. "You are beautiful when you laugh."

"You're not so bad with a smile on your face either."

We weren't two minutes into lunch when my phone rang. I glanced at the readout and saw Vincent's name. Biting my lip, I wondered if I should answer. With Gran's words in my mind about not letting anything interrupt my time with Ethan, I silenced the call and stowed the phone in my purse.

"One of your partners?" Ethan asked, without looking up.

"What makes you think that?" I asked.

"If it were your grandmother, you'd pick up, and it doesn't sound like your mother would call, so that leaves your partners." He still didn't look up.

It was depressing, but true. "I have other friends." I couldn't put much conviction into the statement. My other friends were work-related as well. "But yes, it was." I really didn't have much of a life outside of my job.

"And it was Vincent." It wasn't a question that Ethan asked.

Instant tension started to fill me. Frowning, I was ready to ask how Ethan knew, but he beat me to the punch.

"If it was Logan, you probably would have answered. Since he lives next to your grandmother, you'd worry. If it were Rider... well, I don't think he'd call right now."

After Vincent had spent a few nights at my house, he had become a sore spot between Ethan and me. Ethan had understood why he was there. Someone was trying to kill me after all. He didn't seem too upset about the situation, but he wasn't happy about it, either. It was a good thing Ethan didn't know that my broken soul was caused by Vincent, or that we shared a piece of each other's souls. I don't think he would handle that news well.

Instead of answering, I went back to eating.

"It's not going to bother me if you call him back," Ethan said.

I knew that was a lie, so I shrugged it off. "Whatever it is, he can wait until after lunch."

"And if it's work, or otherwise important?"

"I've been stood down." Those words grated on my nerves so I threw out other excuses. "Plus, I'm hundreds of miles away. Even if it's important, there's nothing I could do."

We finished lunch, mostly in silence. Ethan and I each tried to bring up other topics, but our conversation had fallen flat.

After Ethan paid for lunch, we walked out and he put his arm around me, pulling me close to his side. I leaned into him, feeling comforted by his closeness. He appeared relaxed, but I didn't open the Path to check how he was really feeling. I wasn't sure it was something I wanted to know. Besides, it felt invasive. It would be worse than snooping through his phone or reading his email.

"We only have a few more things to get for the cabin. I'll run to the store and pick them up, and give you a chance to call your partner," Ethan said.

When I tensed again, Ethan stopped and enveloped me in a hug. "I'm not worried about it."

There was a part of me that wanted to let it drop, but of course, I needled deeper. "But it's something that still bothers you."

"I'm not upset with you or him. I'm angry with myself."

The questioning look I had must have been obvious.

"If I hadn't walked out after you told me, well, everything..."

I winced. It had been a mistake telling him the way that I had. Mythological creatures, my powers, my broken soul, even the fact that broken pieces of other souls had stuck to me. He had that dropped on him all at once. It was no wonder he had walked out.

"Then we would have been on firmer ground," he continued. "I feel guilty that it wasn't me that stayed with you that night."

"No one knew that Einar would come to my house," I said.

"No, but I knew someone had tried to hurt you, and someone had sent you a dead rabbit. Granted, I didn't know it came back to life, but that's beside the point. Vincent knew that someone was out to get you and he wasn't willing to take the chance of leaving you alone. That should have been me."

I hadn't really thought of it in those terms. I'm pretty sure that didn't make things any better. In fact, it sounded worse. "Because he's my work partner, nothing else."

Ethan chuckled, but it sounded weighed down. "For some reason, I can't picture him staying the night with Rider or Logan."

"I wouldn't bet on that," I said. "I would stay with any of them if I thought something might happen."

"That's because you are you." Ethan hugged me again. "And it wouldn't surprise me if you camped out on their doorstep if they wouldn't let you inside."

Since I couldn't deny it, I only shrugged in response.

"Know that my problem is with me, not your partner," Ethan said. "Besides, he was the one that told you to give me a chance."

"He did, didn't he?" Remembering that lightened my mood considerably.

"He even talked to me once or twice about you."

"He did?" That took me by surprise.

"Yes, so call him back, see what's going on, and I'll go get our supplies."

It hadn't been the best place for the conversation, but I felt buoyant when Ethan walked away.

Not worrying about the messages, I returned Vincent's call.

Vincent didn't bother with greetings. "Cass, we're still hours away. Were you able to get everything we need?"

"What?" Why didn't I listen to the messages? "Of course you're hours away. Why am I getting you things?"

He was quiet for a moment on the other end. "I'll start from the beginning."

CHAPTER

TWO

"Logan's on special assignment out west," Vincent said. "He reached out to me this morning for a favor, but I think he left a message with you as well. An old friend of his needs help."

"Is it someone we know?" I'm not sure why I asked the question. As far as I could remember, I hadn't met any of Logan's friends, except the people we worked with.

"No, but it's one of the Lost," Vincent said.

"Why didn't he call AIR? They have to have a branch in this area somewhere."

"Logan was adamant that we don't call AIR in on this. Since the three of us are off work, he's asking us to help out until he can get here. He's trusting us to keep it off the record until his friend is safe."

I wasn't sure if this was more of Logan's paranoia about the office knowing too much, but in the end, it didn't matter. "We can do that for Logan. Who are we helping?"

"There's a bigfoot about a hundred miles north of you," Vincent said.

"I thought they all moved out of the country."

"That's why this needs to stay off the record."

"I see," I said, "and what's going on with him?"

"He's being hunted."

"If he's been hiding out for this long, surely he can hide from some hunter in the woods."

"Not this one," Vincent said. "We don't have many details, but he's been forced to leave his home. Now he's on the run."

The details weren't adding up. "Is there something special about the hunter?"

"That's really all we know," Vincent said. "There's not much to go on, and we can't get in touch with Logan's friend. We have to wait for him to get to a place where he can contact us."

"Is there a plan?" I asked.

"We're starting at his house and spreading out from there. Listen, Logan wanted to have you on this, but I know you have other things going on right now. You don't have to join us. We were hoping you could pick up some supplies and meet us at this guy's house so we can get a quick start."

I looked into the store window and saw Ethan at the register. "No, if Logan needs my help, of course I'll help. I'll need to talk to Ethan first. So, um, it sounds like Rider's with you?"

"He is."

"He's only been out of bed for a few days. Is he..." I broke off. If I asked if he was up for this, it would sound like he couldn't handle it. That would only make our strained friendship worse, so I shifted subjects. "Um, how's your hand?"

"It's holding up. It'll be in a cast for a while longer, though."

"I'll make sure there's pain reliever on the list somewhere."

"Thanks, Cass. I'll text you the directions to the bigfoot's house," Vincent said.

"Does he have a name?" I asked.

"From what Logan said, this guy isn't much of a people person. He'll answer to Harry, though."

"Does he know we're coming?" I asked.

"He knows that Logan is sending someone. We're hoping he contacts Logan again, so he knows who we are."

"I hope so," I said. "I'll get the stuff and meet you."

"You don't have to cancel your vacation," Vincent said. "Talk to Ethan first."

"Sure. I'll be on the lookout for your text. The list of stuff is in the messages, right?"

"Yes."

"I'll call you back if I still have a signal. Otherwise, I'll meet you."

After Vincent hung up, I listened to the messages. I had barely gotten through Logan's call explaining the situation, when Ethan came out of the store.

"How's everything back home?" Ethan asked.

"Back home, things are okay, but something has come up."

Ethan raised an eyebrow, but waited for me to explain.

I gave him all the details that I had. "I'm sorry about this, Ethan, but I really think they could use my help."

He nodded. "I get it."

Looking at him, I could tell he really meant what he said. "I'm glad you understand."

"I do. It sounds like we'll be going backcountry. We're in the mountains so the terrain could be rough in a few places. Let's look at the list they sent you."

"We?" Crap, why did I let that pop out? I rushed to cover the awkwardness. "I mean, you know you don't have to help us with this, right?"

"Would you rather I didn't come?" He asked.

"That's not what I'm saying-"

"Good, because I was coming with you anyway."

The corner of my mouth curved up. "You were, were you?"

"You bet. Your partners have had a tough time lately. They'll need the help. Besides," he gave me a devilish grin, "I still can't picture you spending the night in the woods."

We picked up everything that Vincent asked us to get. Thankfully, he told us what he already had as well, so we knew what to add. Ethan even added a few items to the list.

When I called Vincent back, I held my breath, unsure of how to tell him Ethan would be joining us. Luckily, I was able to leave a message instead of speaking with him in person. I made it clear that Ethan and I would meet them at Harry's house, and that we had all the equipment needed for the four of us to wander the wilderness.

"I'm really sorry about this," I told Ethan hours later and for the thousandth time since we closed up our cabin.

"It'll be interesting," Ethan said. "I'll get to see you and your team at work, and you and I will still get to spend time together. Besides, it's Bigfoot. If I'm lucky, I'll get the chance to see something very few people have actually seen."

"This isn't exactly work sanctioned or anything," I said.

"You know what I mean."

"I know." And that very thought was making me apprehensive. He sounded as though seeing us in action, a Reader, a werewolf, and a Walker, was going to be a show. "But schlepping around the backcountry, sleeping in the trees or on the ground isn't exactly a vacation, and it could be dangerous."

"I've been in worse situations than going to pick up a poacher," Ethan said.

"He's attempting to kill someone," I corrected. "Harry's a person, not an animal."

"We know that, but does the hunter?" Ethan asked.

I didn't know how to answer the question, so I ignored it. "We're almost there."

"That's good," Ethan said, "because we're about out of road."

It was true. The gravel on our gravel road had disappeared about a mile ago. What we were driving on was more of a rut through the woods than a road.

"Do you see a house anywhere?" I asked.

"No, but there's a big truck up ahead," Ethan said.

"Do you think that belongs to the guy we're looking for?" I asked.

"Let's go find out." Ethan pulled to a stop behind a large black 4x4 with dark tinted windows. The truck gleamed as though it had just left a showroom floor, and since it had temporary tags instead of license plates, it very well could have.

"Wait here." Ethan didn't shut off the car, but he opened the door and stepped out.

"What do you mean wait here?" I pushed my car door open, got out, and then glared at Ethan over the top of the car.

"I meant-"

The driver side of the truck opened and Ethan tensed. I didn't reach for the Path, but I readied my mind to make the jump.

When I saw Rider get out of the driver's side of the truck, I was glad I hadn't reached for the Path. He was one of the rare people that could tell when I opened the Path. I didn't want him to think that I was.

Rider's dark eyes caught mine and he looked hesitant for a

moment. Or maybe I imagined that. Within a blink, his eyes hardened and his gaze swept to Ethan.

My heart fell. I hadn't realized I was anxious about seeing Rider again until he looked away. It would be useful to know what I did wrong so I could fix it and get my best friend back.

The passenger door opened and Vincent got out. Appearing more animated than usual, Vincent looked from his partner to me and shook his head before joining Ethan and me.

"Ethan," Vincent nodded, "it's good to see you here. Sorry to take you away from your vacation."

"Anything for a friend, right?" Ethan said.

I didn't think he meant it as a question, but Vincent took it as one.

"We can use all the help we can get," Vincent said. "Let's see what we've got so we can start."

Vincent wasn't wrong about needing the extra help. Even with Rider keeping his distance, I could see that he was paler than normal. It was hard to believe that he was even up and moving after being shot in the chest only last week.

Vincent walked by me and I tugged his arm to hold him up while Ethan went to open the trunk of the car. That small connection with Vincent was enough to feel a surge between us. He stopped and I yanked my hand back before our souls sought each other out.

"Sorry," I said automatically. Ever since he had tried to kill me last fall, I had a piece of his soul, and he had a piece of mine. Vincent was adamant that we shouldn't see each other on a personal level, so we avoided acknowledging our connection.

Seeing the look in his eye, I decided that Vincent might not be as adamant about our relationship as I thought.

"We picked up everything you asked for," Ethan said while rummaging around in the trunk.

It was too late for Vincent and me now, so I pushed it out of my head.

"How's your hand?" I asked while trying covertly to increase the amount of space between us.

"It's getting better," Vincent said.

"And your partner?" I dropped my voice, but I knew it wouldn't matter. Rider could probably be half a mile away and still hear a whisper.

"Also getting better," Vincent said. "Why don't you two ready the gear we brought and Ethan and I will bring the rest over."

I cast a nervous look at Rider. "Sure."

Rider already had the tailgate of the truck pulled down when I approached. My stomach felt twisted and I bit my lip. What kind of reaction would I get from Rider?

"This is a nice truck," I said. "Is it yours?"

Rider didn't look at me, but jumped into the back of the truck and started pushing stuff onto the tailgate. "I have purchased the vehicle."

"That's, um, it's nice," I repeated. "And you look good. Better, I mean, than last week."

"I heal fast," Rider said.

"Yeah." I twisted my hands and decided to say what I wanted to say. "Listen, I wanted to let you know that-"

"Here's one bag," Vincent said, coming up beside me. He caught my eye and shook his head in the smallest fraction.

The words 'I'm sorry' died in my throat.

"Right," I breathed. Not the way to go. Rider and Vincent must be getting closer to the friend stage if Vincent knew enough to stop me. Friendship means a lot to a werewolf.

At least I thought it did. If I apologized for getting him shot it would be implying weakness, or that he couldn't hold up his end of the friendship.

"Right," I said again, louder, "what do we have?"

Vincent and Ethan began to organize our supplies. It took a remarkably small amount of time to fit everything like a puzzle into four bags, each item finding its own little spot. As if by unspoken communication, they had decided to make my bag lighter than the others were.

"Try this on," Ethan said. "Let's adjust the straps."

"It looked like it could fit a bit more," I said.

"If we need the space," Ethan said, "we'll add more."

When he put the bag on my back, though, I was glad it wasn't any heavier.

Ethan moved around in front of me and adjusted the shoulder straps. While his concentration was on the bag, my eyes were on him.

He caught me watching him and smiled. Using my shoulder straps, he pulled me closer. "I'm not sure how long we'll be out here, but maybe we'll get the chance to see those early morning stars."

"Because that worked out so well for us before," I smirked.

"It's fun trying, though." Ethan winked at me and then gave me a quick kiss before stepping away.

My partners were very pointedly not looking in our direction.

"So," I cleared my throat, "where does the Lost live? I don't see a house."

"Logan said it's not far," Vincent said.

"Harry left on foot?" I asked.

"That's what we understand," Vincent said. "I thought we'd start at the house and go from there."

Rider jumped down from the back of the truck and picked up his bag with one hand. It had been the heaviest pack by far, but he swung it around as I would a purse.

"This way," Rider said, and then set out through the under-growth without making a sound.

Vincent and Ethan followed, and I brought up the rear.

"You guys are sure we have everything we need, right?" I couldn't help but feel apprehensive when we moved away from the vehicles.

"We're good for three or four days, assuming we find a water source," Ethan said. "Any longer than that and we'll have to catch dinner."

Three or four days? "Um, do you think we'll be out here that long?" I tried to make my voice sound casual. It's possible I might even have succeeded, but Vincent felt the tension under my voice. As a side effect of sharing a small piece of my soul, it's possible he always would.

CHAPTER

THREE

"We hope it won't take that long," Vincent said, "but we are tracking a bigfoot, or someone hunting one anyway. They're well-known for being elusive."

Ethan chuckled.

"What?" I asked, worried he had caught my trepidation and found it amusing.

"It's just...I can't believe I'm going cross-country looking for bigfoot," Ethan said. He laughed again. "With my girlfriend, no less."

I grinned, enjoying the fact that Ethan referred to me as his girlfriend, but then I felt an undercurrent of tension start to build. My smile turned weak and I reached for the Path.

"Over here," Rider called.

Without making the jump to the Path, I quickened my pace to catch up to Ethan. He looked excited, thrilled even. The feeling must have come from one of the others. I let it drop and concentrated on the small shack in front of us.

"It looks like a shed," Ethan said.

Rider walked around the building then looked around the forest. Shadows were growing darker and deeper, but the sun hadn't given up on the day yet.

Vincent knocked on a piece of sheet metal that appeared to be the makeshift door. "Harry?"

The shed was tiny. Would a bigfoot actually live in a place like that? The thought that Harry, Logan's friend and one of the last bigfoot in the Northern Hemisphere, lived in such a flimsy little shack made my heart ache.

Vincent rattled the metal. "Ethan, do you want to help me with this? I think we can move it to the side and-"

"Do not go inside," Rider said without turning back to the dilapidated pile of metal.

Vincent took a step back, but still had eyes on the shed. "He's not in there, but we should at least check."

"I do not think that Harry lives in the metal house," Rider said.

"Do you think he lives in the open?" I asked.

Rider didn't answer, but he seemed to be concentrating on something, so I tried not to take it personally. He shook his head, rolled his shoulders, and then turned in a circle, scanning the woods.

"What are you thinking?" Vincent asked after Rider completed his circle. "We're still in the dark."

Rider frowned and looked at the sky. "The sun is still out and the shadows are not deep enough to leave you in the dark."

"He means that you seem to understand something that we're missing," I said with a wistful smile, missing my friend even though he stood in front of me.

"He has confused the smell," Rider said. "I assume it was

Harry that did this. The smells lead to here, but they are mangled. Meant to lure."

"You mean it's a trap?" Ethan asked.

"I do not know if it is meant to be malicious or misleading," Rider said, "but Harry does not live here."

"But he probably lives near here. This is where Logan sent us as well," Vincent said.

I started looking closer to the area surrounding us as well. Vincent was right. Logan wouldn't have sent us knowingly into a trap, so Harry's actual house had to be around here somewhere.

"The smell is too thick to find a trail. I can circle out until I find the correct scent," Rider said.

"We could split up," Ethan suggested. "Each walk in a different direction to see what we find."

Rider's gaze flickered in my direction for a moment so brief that I might have imagined it. "There are other smells. Bear, wild cats." Rider turned to Vincent. "The woods are full of predators."

"Most of those animals aren't going to bother us unless we startle them," Ethan said.

Knowing where the conversation was heading, I closed my eyes. Predators reacted poorly to me, and they would go out of their way to cause trouble, but I didn't want Ethan to be reminded of this fact. With my eyes closed, I mentally stretched myself to the edge of my knowledge of the world as we know it. The border between my mind and the Path was getting crowded. Fragments of my soul and others gathered there. Luckily, my own soul knew it belonged and kept the other pieces in check.

Ignoring the glittery shards, I jumped over the chaos and into the Path. Holding back as much of the power as I could while still being effective, I opened my eyes. A shimmering overlay streamed through the landscape. Memories of expended energy lay in front of me, ready to be read.

"In most cases this-" Rider broke off what he was saying mid-sentence. I'm not sure what he experienced when I read the Path, but he could always tell when I opened myself up to the vivid world of swirling color.

Everything leaves a trace in our world, and as a Reader, I was skilled in interpreting what was left behind, although, in rare cases, I was also able to glimpse Paths that hadn't yet been laid. It's understandable that I might catch something that hadn't happened yet, since I was born into a long line of psychics.

Here, I was firmly in the present. I avoided looking at the others. It always seemed like an intrusion to look too closely at my partners or Ethan if there was no need to know what they were feeling.

Pale streams of green and brown wound around the land-scape. Animals, and more of them than I would expect, even for the forest, had made trails everywhere.

The others had gone silent and I could feel their eyes on me. I ignored the animal imprints and concentrated on the others. There was a trail left behind where someone had walked repeatedly, burning their movements into the Path. I assumed that was Harry. Besides the Paths of my partners, there were two others that stood out. I took note of them, but knowing that we were running out of daylight, I concentrated again on Harry.

"He walked through here regularly," I said. "I agree with Rider. It's as if he purposefully made the area remember him. But I don't see any sign he entered the shack."

"Is there any way to tell where he might live?" Ethan asked.

"It's strange. I see places he may have entered and exited

the area, but they're all faint. There is, however, a brighter Path that way." I pointed deeper into the woods.

"So he came and went from that direction more often?" Vincent asked.

Rider went to the area I indicated and I joined him.

"Not exactly." I studied the area where this brighter Path came into contact with the repeated efforts of Harry's misdirection. "It looks like this Path was made by someone else."

"I agree," Rider said. "This scent is unlike the others."

"But it melds with the Path that I presume to be Harry's." I moved my hand through the Path. "It flows from here, straight into the other Path."

"So it's someone Harry knows, or maybe it's our hunter," Ethan said.

I studied the Path and thought it over. "Is it possible for someone to change their smell?"

"People use things that hide or cover their scent," Rider said, "but it does not alter it. Your smell is the only one that I have seen change."

Ignoring the comments on my own smell, I went on. "It's sort of the same with Paths. People have an underlying Path that's their own. It can change shape and color based on emotion, but the Path still remembers that it was the same person. Their core imprint is still there."

"I understand what you're saying," Vincent said, "but I'm not sure I understand the context. Why is the base smell or Path relevant here?"

As I focused on the bright Path and where it entered the other, I found what I was looking for. "I think both Paths are Harry's. When he entered this area, one Path doesn't just bump into or run over the other, it flows into it, and...it's hard to explain. It kind of twists and becomes the other Path."

"So, Harry comes to this area, alters himself somehow, makes sure this area stands out, and then what?" Ethan asked.

"I think he left the area in different directions each time. Maybe to chase the animals away? Or to confuse anyone who can smell him or see the Path," I amended.

"It's starting to get dark," Vincent said. "Let's follow this and see if we can find Harry's house. If we don't, tomorrow morning we can come back here and take another look."

"Sounds like a plan," Ethan said.

Rider and I took the lead. Rider's eyesight was almost as good at night as it was during the day, and with the Path open, light filled my world.

While I was absorbed in the Path, Rider stalked ahead, but together, we were making decent time at a quick pace. Looking up, trees swung back and forth in the wind leaving impressive wisps of color, pale greens, yellows, and in one case gray, trailing behind each sway until the Path swept it away.

It was fascinating to watch. At least, until Rider swung out his hand and I walked into the unmovable limb face first.

I stumbled back, but caught myself before falling and glared at Rider's back. "What was that for?"

Rider ignored the question and stood stock still.

"What happened?" Ethan asked.

"I..." I sighed at my own inattentiveness. "Never mind."

"Someone else came through here," Rider said.

Paying closer attention to Rider, I saw that he had stopped in front of a set of intersecting Paths in front of us.

"I saw these two Paths back at the shed," I said.

"I smell only one," Rider said.

"One looks like it could be a person. It's a bit clouded to be sure. The other looks like an animal, but more substantial," I said.

"I do not know what that means," Rider said.

"Animals without complex thought leave lighter, almost ghosted trails. They have simple emotions, and only a few of them, so their Path isn't as dense. People, on the other hand, are more complicated. The Path remembers us in a more solid way. In this case, the pattern in the Path is simple, but solid."

"I do not smell an animal with the new person," Rider said. "Did it go through at the same time?"

"Around the same time, I think," I said. "I'd have to follow the Path back to the past to be sure."

"I don't think that will be necessary," Vincent said carefully. "It's getting late and we've been on this trail for a while now."

Meaning he thought I had been Reading too long already. I could argue and say I felt fine, but in truth, I was a bit worn.

"Which trail do we follow?" I asked.

"Harry's," Vincent said. "If the new one goes in a different direction, it could be unrelated. We should start by checking Harry's house, if we can find it. Rider, do you want to lead the way?"

I rolled my eyes, taking the hint. Rider didn't move, so I closed my eyes and concentrated on pushing the Path aside.

The Path fought back.

Holding back the torrent of energy and letting only a small piece through had been easy this time. I had expected releasing the Path to be the same way, but my power rebelled and stayed in the brightly colored world. Taking a deep breath, I steadied myself and concentrated. Paths pushed in on me from every side. Even with my eyes shut, I could see the rapidly flowing stream of information. Little by little, I closed up the dam of color and made the mental leap back into the normal world.

When I opened my eyes the world was dark, and I swayed on my feet, more tired than I realized. Rider put a hand on my shoulder to steady me. When I looked up into his face, I could see that his mouth was set in a hard line, but he wasn't even looking at me.

Did that mean he was trying to be all business, or was he being a friend, but not letting it show? The whole situation with Rider was getting too confusing, so I tossed the thought aside.

"I'm good," I said. "Let's get moving."

Cool mountain air started to weave through the night. The day hadn't been too hot, but it was summer and the fresh air felt good. Usually, I have decent night vision, but I was still light-blinded from the Path. Tripping over tree branches and stepping in unseen holes wasn't what you would call a good time.

"I think we need to stop for the night," I said after stumbling over another tree root. "We could walk by the house and never see it."

"Rider, any idea how old the trail is you're following now?" Vincent asked.

Rider stopped. "Five days, give or take a half day."

"Then we still haven't found Harry's most recent departure from the area." Vincent unclasped a buckle on his backpack. "We'll stop for tonight, but leave as early as we can in the morning."

When I took off the backpack, the air hitting my back felt cold, and I realized I was covered in sweat. Vincent took my bag and lined it up with the others. I arched my back, stretching out the muscles that had been weighed down throughout the day. When I looked around, everyone else was hard at work.

Camping wasn't a skill I possessed, and I was thoroughly clueless as to what I should be doing. What had we done last time?

Looking over, I saw Rider twisting around a small ball of material. Our hammocks. That was something I was at least a little familiar with.

I felt nervous approaching Rider, which I hated. "Can I help you with your hammock?"

"I thought this one was yours," he mumbled, turning the fabric over.

"Maybe," I said. "I can grab one end and-"

"You should help Vincent," Rider said.

"Oh, yeah." There was no way to keep the hurt from my voice, but I tried my hardest. He may as well have slapped me in the face. "I'll do that."

Rider didn't look my way, but in a low voice he added. "He could use the assistance due to his hand."

"Right." A small hope buoyed my heart. "I'll help him."

He didn't say anything else, so I wasn't sure if he added the detail for my benefit or for Vincent's. Either way, he wasn't sending me away to get rid of me.

I knelt down next to Vincent by the backpacks and looked around. "Where's Ethan?"

Vincent pointed up. A rope dangled in the air and as I followed it up, I saw Ethan lying out on a large branch.

"How did he even get up there?" I asked.

"He was there before I realized what he was doing. Take this," Vincent handed me the end of a rope, "hold it here and here."

Holding the line, I watched Vincent make a strange knot.

That was followed by three more. Soon, Ethan was out of the tree. Our backpacks were dangling from branches and Rider had our hammock stretched tightly between trees.

"I've never camped without a tent," Ethan said, walking up behind me and putting his arms around me.

Leaning back into him, relishing in the closeness, I eyed my bed for the night, which was about chest-height off the ground.

"I've never camped with a tent," I said.

"Not once?" Ethan asked.

"Well, Gran set one up in her backyard once," I said. "And we spent part of the night out there. I'm not sure that counts, though."

"Probably not," Ethan said.

I could hear the laughter that he was holding back in his voice. I nudged him in the ribs with my elbow, and he let out a chuckle.

"Next time, we'll try a tent." He hugged me closer from behind and spoke low into my ear. "We can share a sleeping bag."

"There are four sleeping bags." Rider sounded sincere in his statement. "You will not have to share."

Luckily, it was dark because my face turned four different shades of red. Ethan seemed as tongue-tied as I was.

I heard a muffled voice and turned to see Vincent talking to Rider.

Rider's face creased in confusion. "I do not understand. We slept with each other the last time we spent the night outside, and we did not share sleeping bags."

Ethan went very still.

"No," I said, pulling out of Ethan's arms and turning to Rider, though my words were more for Ethan's sake. "We slept next to each other, not with each other. There is a distinct difference."

Vincent was whispering once again to Rider, and I crossed my arms, glaring at the two.

"Oh, that is very different." Rider said. He was quieter this time, but we could still hear him clearly. "Should I get rid of one of the sleeping bags?"

Closing my eyes, I rubbed my forehead and tried to wish myself far away. Then I realized that Vincent had not replied. Looking up, I could see that they were waiting for an answer from Ethan or me.

What on earth are they thinking?

"That's a nice offer, Rider." I worked to keep my voice level and not look at Ethan. "But I think we're okay."

Rider shrugged and turned back to his hammock.

Finally, I bit my lip and looked at Ethan. He was grinning and shaking his head.

Relief washed over me, but I tried not to let it show. There were so many ways for Ethan to take the conversation. Amused wasn't what I had expected.

I put my hand on my hip in feigned accusation. "What are you smiling about?"

He wrapped an arm around me and kissed me in reply. "This is going to be an interesting vacation." Louder, he added, "I can take first watch if you all would like."

I hadn't even thought of watches, but I kept my mouth shut, not wanting to admit the mental slip.

"It's going to be a short night. We probably only need two," Vincent said. "I'll take the second."

"Wake me if you need me," Rider said.

"Same here," I said.

It took ages for me to fall asleep. On the plus side, the nightmares that had been plaguing me for what seemed like weeks didn't have time to set in before Vincent woke. We were in a hurry, but before he woke us up, he had boiled water for coffee, for which everyone was grateful. I wouldn't say that it perked us up, but it had us back on the search, Rider leading the way.

Fog filled the mountains, chilling the air and making the predawn light even dimmer than you'd expect. Mentally, I blamed my shorter legs for falling behind the others, but I kept someone in sight, even if it meant speed walking off and on.

When the sun crested the horizon, causing a pale yellow glow, Rider stopped. "The trail ends here," he said.

"There's no house here," I said, stating the obvious. "Does the smell change here?"

"No," Rider said.

"The fog is covering a lot," Vincent said. "Fan out and look around. Don't go far."

I turned back the way we came, but I didn't go anywhere. The sound of twigs breaking and leaves rustling announced the others leaving. Once the sound turned pillowy, I closed my eyes and stretched for the Path.

I could have done this while they were here, but I didn't want to contradict Vincent. Why he hadn't suggested I look was a mystery to me.

Vivid, robust color entered my world again. The roar was stronger this time, since I wasn't able to hold back as much power as I had yesterday. The fog was making things interesting. Where the clouds shifted and twirled, a secondary layer moved with it, like a couple dancing.

Mesmerized, I watched the fog with its shimmering partner until I caught sight of the Path we had been following. I followed it back to where Rider stopped. He wasn't wrong. If this was Harry, he was here, and then he wasn't.

Above us, the treetops were visible as the fog started to

burn away. There were no limbs or branches to jump to, so Harry didn't go up. If he had died, either his body would be here, or the Path of his body would be. That only left one direction.

I slid off my backpack before bending over and dragging my fingers across the ground. It was dirt and grass, like you would expect, but when I tried to scrape up some soil, it didn't budge. Moving my hands around the forest floor, I searched for the spots where the ground was different. It didn't take long to find what I was looking for. A tree root, which you would expect to be immovable, but in this case, was a handle.

"I think I've found it," I called to the others. It crossed my mind that I could dig a little further, make sure it was a trap door, and even open it up. But what if Harry wasn't the only person who lived there? Or what if someone else moved in after he had left?

Besides, when I tried to lift it, it didn't move, even when I put some strength behind it.

When all three had come back into view, I pointed out what I suspected was Harry's door.

Rider dumped his backpack and pulled the root. It swung up, taking a large chunk of the ground with it. Below was a large hole, with a ladder dropping straight into darkness. What I had come to think of as Harry's Path went down. With that confirmed, I closed my eyes and pushed the Path away. This time, it fell away with no effort.

"Nice work, Cass," Vincent said. He took a flashlight out of his backpack and shined it into the gloom. The rock wall of the hole glittered as the light struck it, but I didn't see the ground.

"Well," Ethan said, "the ladder has to lead somewhere." He set aside his pack and took out a headlamp and another flashlight. "Might as well make myself useful. I'll go first."

"Are you sure?" I asked before I could stop myself.

Ethan only smiled at me and winked. Turning to the others, he asked, "Did this guy have any pets or anything?"

"Not that we are aware of," Vincent said. He was using a careful tone and I could see the unease in the corners of his eyes.

"Should we all go down?" I asked.

"No," Vincent said.

"After I've checked out where this thing lands, I'll holler up." Ethan put the flashlight in his back pocket.

"Wait." Vincent leaned over Harry's entrance and yelled into the hole. "Harry, you in there?" He paused. "Anyone?" Pause. "Okay, we're friendly, and we're coming down." Turning to Ethan, he asked, "Are you armed?"

Ethan patted his hip where his concealed holster rested. "I am."

"Good, run if you have to, but don't shoot anything."

Ethan was scrambling down the ladder faster than I had anticipated.

"If it's clear," Vincent said, "one of you needs to wait up here with the bags."

"I will stay," Rider said.

Vincent nodded. "Are you two armed?"

"Yes," Rider said.

They both looked at me. "I was on vacation." It was my only defense and I was grabbing onto it.

Twinges of aggravation leapt off Vincent's face. I wasn't sure if Rider could see them, but to me, they were obvious.

"You," Vincent said, "of all people, should be carrying a weapon at all times."

"I have a knife." It was lame, but at least I had something. A part of me wanted to argue that the Path could be my weapon if I needed it, but they knew what that did to me, and they knew it wouldn't last.

"I've found the bottom." Ethan's voice echoed up the hole.

Leaning over, I could see his light moving in a circle.

Vincent shook his head. "Stick to one of us at all times."

My eyes narrowed automatically.

"Please," Vincent added before I could say anything.

I rolled my eyes and shook my head. "It's not like I'm going to run off into the woods on my own."

"It's all clear," Ethan yelled.

"Ladies first," Vincent said.

When was the last time I had been on a ladder? How had Ethan gotten onto the thing?

I sat down and swung my legs into the empty air, feeling around until I found the ladder. Vincent held out his hand and I wordlessly grabbed it and lowered myself into the hole. The rungs of the ladder were cold metal. It didn't take long for me to wish I had turned on my headlamp before starting down. Looking up, I saw Vincent following me, and then I looked down, which was a mistake. Nothing was below and my head felt like it was slowly starting to spin.

FIVE

Closing my eyes, I took a few steadying breaths. There was no way I could stop here. Ethan was below me; Vincent was above me. It was okay. I was all right.

It's not as though I was afraid of the dark, but it changes things when you know what could be lurking in the unknown.

When I opened my eyes, I almost looked down again, but I caught myself in time. Concentrating on the rung in front of me, I went down. With each step, I told myself there was a bottom to this ladder. Ethan wouldn't have lied about that. My hands were starting to get stiff. How was I going to get back up this thing?

My foot struck dirt instead of another rung and I looked around. The glow of Ethan's flashlight wasn't far off, but was pointed in another direction. I flipped on my headlamp and looked up. No problem, I told myself. That was easy. Going up would be a piece of cake.

I stepped out of Vincent's way and looked around at the rough stone walls.

"This isn't your usual cave," I said, running my hand over the rock.

"You're right about that," Ethan said, taking my hand. He looked like a kid on Christmas morning. "You've gotta see this."

Ethan led me down the hall. Vincent didn't follow right away. I saw his flashlight checking the shadows before turning to join us. We reached a corner and Ethan pointed his light down another passageway.

Except it was a hallway. The stone had been chiseled to this point. Once you turned down the hall, it was as smooth as glass. Our lights glinted off the surface. There was a wooden door set into the wall at the end. At least it looked like wood. It was, in fact, carved to look like a tree that happened to hold a doorway.

"Wait," Vincent said, catching up to us.

I hadn't even realized I was walking towards the door. "What?"

"Harry apparently discouraged visitors," Vincent said. "There may be traps through here."

"I checked the hallway," Ethan said. "It looks like he did set one, but it had already been sprung. The door looks amazing, but I have no idea how to tell if it's booby trapped or not. It looks like it leads to Narnia, not someone's home."

I chuckled. It really was a beautiful door, and it was entirely out of place.

Vincent frowned. "Cass, what do you see?"

The carving of the tree seemed to sing out to me, but Vincent was right. I closed my eyes and jumped into the Path. The dim cave was now brightly lit for my eyes. Ignoring Ethan and Vincent, I found Harry's Path and followed it. Unfortunately, it headed in the opposite direction of the tree. Around another small, tight corner, there was door set into the stone.

"I wonder what he has behind the other door." I said.

"Let's not find out," Ethan said.

Vincent knocked before opening the door. He had to duck before going through, as did Ethan. After pushing the Path away, I walked into Harry's home.

You could tell it was a home. The ceilings were high and a few pieces of wooden furniture had makeshift cushions that looked like they had been woven out of vines. Unfortunately, what could pass as a chair was turned over, and in the corner, it looked like something had been set on fire.

There were only four rooms, and we cleared them quickly. Once we knew we were alone, we began a more thorough inspection. Harry had one wall that had been full of books, but they were mostly littered around on the floor now. I stooped and picked one up. The green cloth cover was ripped, but the book was largely intact. It was a small volume and the cover was unreadable. Opening to the first page, I found the title, *Hamlet*.

"Alas, poor Yorick," I mumbled and closed the book. A deep sadness welled up. This was the middle of nowhere. Harry lived out here, alone, not bothering anyone. Alone with his massive collection of books, and someone came and tried to track him like an animal.

Why?

Because he was different. One of the Lost from another dimension, living here, and trying to make a life for himself. My job was to keep him and all the others like him, safe and hidden from the world, but someone stumbled onto a bigfoot, and now Harry was running for his life.

"Cass?"

Sniffing, I turned to see Vincent and Ethan watching me. "Sorry, I'm fine. We need to get moving."

They didn't budge and continued to stare.

"What?" I asked. An uneasy feeling was creeping up. I had sniffed a few times, but it's not as though I had been crying or making a spectacle of myself.

"You were, well, whistling, I guess," Ethan said, a worried look on his face.

"Was I?" I asked. Then I crossed my arms. "So what?"

"It was sad, but..." Ethan trailed off, so I turned to Vincent.

He was doing his best to keep a blank look on his face.

"What?" I asked, louder this time.

"It wasn't you," Vincent said.

"What does that mean?" I asked.

Vincent looked leery. "It doesn't matter right now. There's another exit. Rider is bringing our bags down. We'll leave from here."

When Vincent stepped out of the room I was left with Ethan, his eyes still wide.

I glared at him before looking away and pretending to concentrate on books. Ethan took his time, but he moved over to me and took my hand.

"Everything okay?" he asked.

"You tell me."

He shook his head. "It must be the way the room made you sound. It was... well, it wasn't normal."

"What's normal?" I muttered.

A low ominous growl rumbled through the room and echoed, making it sound like it was coming from everywhere at once. The hairs on the back of my neck rose as the noise sunk into me and I froze on the spot.

"Rider?" It was half a question and half a yell from Vincent.

Slowly, I turned, not wanting to make any sudden movements. Ethan stood in my way, but I could see around him to where Vincent stood in front of Rider. In the dim light I could see Rider's dark eyes staring menacingly in my direction.

Nothing moved in those hollowed-out rooms as we stared at each other.

"Enough!" Vincent yelled. When he looked at each of us in turn I saw that his eyes were black. "We don't have time for this."

Rider rolled his shoulders and looked away.

"What the hell was that about?" Ethan asked.

I glanced at Rider and shook my head. What had happened? Since I didn't know, there was nothing for me to say.

Rider picked up two bags and stalked out of the room.

"We need to move," Vincent said, not looking at anyone. "I've got your bag, Cass, let's go."

He didn't wait for a reply and walked out. I started to follow him, but Ethan took my arm.

"What was that?" Ethan asked.

Even without the Path I could sense his indignation building.

"I don't know," I snapped, pulling away.

"Is he dangerous?" Ethan asked.

"Rider? He's not going to hurt us. It's probably some sort of werewolf thing."

Ethan looked like he was thinking that over.

"We really need to go," I said.

In a huff, Ethan picked up his bag and left, with me following behind. There was another passage out, and we weren't able to catch up to Vincent and Rider until the cave opened to the forest.

Great, I thought while looking at the others, I'm stuck in the woods with a werewolf, a Walker, and a boyfriend, each of them pissed off. And me? Now that I didn't feel the need to check the shadows for the boogeyman, I didn't know what to think.

No one said a word, but Vincent handed me my pack and Rider shoved a boulder back into its spot blocking the cave. Then we picked up the trail again.

The fog was gone and the sun was beating down with the promise of heat later in the day. Even with no one talking, the air crackled around the men, as though charged. There was nothing I could think of to say that would lighten the mood, so I kept quiet.

The pace Rider set was brisk, but no one voiced any complaints. They seemed too agitated, but I was feeling the press of urgency. When my stomach started growling, I ignored it, not wanting to stall our progress.

It was sometime after noon when Rider stopped. "There is another scent."

"Going in the same direction?" I asked.

"Two are going in the same direction," Rider said.

"Can you tell how far behind we are?" Vincent asked.

"We are gaining ground, but we are almost a day behind Harry, and nine hours behind the new scent," Rider said.

"We've gotta move faster then," I said, adjusting the pack on my back.

Vincent gave each person a quick look. "No, if we go at this any harder, we're not going to be able to keep going."

"I can move quicker on my own," Rider said. It wasn't said in a mean way, but I could tell from the look on Ethan's face that he didn't appreciate the statement.

Even Vincent looked uneasy. "We still don't know what we're getting into. Grab some food out of your pack and we'll eat on the go."

Food sounded divine, but I begrudged the short stop to get the protein bars from the packs. Even when we were on the move again, the food tasted bland and the need to move faster became more intense.

My concentration was split between the ground and Rider, but I looked around the area when I was sure a tree root or stray rock wasn't waiting to trip me up. There was nothing here that indicated people had come in this direction. There was undergrowth in the area, and occasionally a small animal trail connected with our own path, but there were no signs or sounds that people had ever been here.

Up ahead, Rider paused, and then dropped out of sight.

Despite the extreme fatigue setting into my muscles, I jogged ahead and called out, "Rider?"

I stopped at the edge of a rocky ravine. It looked as though a river or creek had pushed its way through eons ago, and left a hollowed-out area before it dried up. Rider looked troubled and was walking back and forth through the area. Vincent came up behind me and watched.

"What's wrong?" Vincent asked.

"The new trail...the hunter, he stopped here last night," Rider said.

"That's good, right?" Vincent asked. "We're catching up."

"It is odd," Rider said.

We waited for a follow-up, but none came.

"What's odd?" I asked.

"There are two here," Rider said.

"Two what?" I asked.

Once again, he didn't answer, but kept walking relentlessly through the area.

"Rider, we're in the dark here," Vincent said.

The werewolf mumbled something, and I caught the word 'light' mixed up in the incoherent words.

Sighing, I dropped my bag and looked around. Ethan had already removed his and was leaning against a tree watching all three of us.

I felt worn to the bone and wasn't in the mood to play word

games or wait for answers. With my head filled with frustration, it was hard to move beyond it and reach the Path, but I managed the feat and looked around.

The flow of the Path around Rider showed the same two Paths I saw the day before. The one Rider could smell and the one he could not. Turning towards the way we came, I saw that the two had been together as we followed. I relayed the information to the others. If anything, Rider looked more upset than before.

"I'm not sure what this means," Vincent said.

"Neither am I," I said, and looked at Rider.

He shrugged, but he had stopped his pacing.

Vincent looked at the sky. "It's not a bad place to stay for the night."

"No!" Rider and I said together.

"Look," I continued, "it's too early to stop."

"A break then," Vincent said.

I looked at him and Ethan. They looked almost as worn as I felt. Rider, however, seemed as good as new.

Rider noticed me assessing him and knew he had an ally. "I do not need to rest."

Biting my lip, I looked at the Path behind us and then ahead. On the other side of the ravine, I could see the two Paths exiting and moving on, following Harry's trail.

"I have a compromise," I said. "We stop and take a break here, but Rider scouts ahead." Vincent looked like he was going to interrupt, but I rushed over to him. "He's not going to get close to anyone, but Harry didn't run cross country in a straight line. Maybe Rider can follow and find us a short cut?"

"Yes," Rider said immediately.

It was evident Vincent didn't think much of the idea, but he was stuck. Being a friend to a werewolf was tricky. Vincent and Rider may not have fully reached that stage yet, but suggesting the werewolf couldn't do this, couldn't do what he thought was his duty, would be a huge insult. I had put Vincent in a bad spot, and from the glare he was giving me, he knew it.

"Don't get too close to anyone," Vincent said.

CHAPTER

SIX

We moved to the other side of the ravine. Rider took food and water, but left his bag behind.

Sitting on the ground, leaning against my pack, I stared at the sky. It didn't take long before the aches in my muscles really started to settle in and make themselves known. I stretched and looked at the others. Ethan had his eyes closed and was leaning against a tree. Vincent was taking in his surroundings, eyeing the terrain as though he thought someone might jump out at us at any moment. There was a pinched look around his eyes that made me rummage around in my bag.

Grabbing the pain reliever, I shook the bottle until Vincent looked my way, and then I tossed it over.

"Thanks." Although he said the words, his voice didn't convey the same meaning. He took the pills, and then looked in the direction Rider had left. "You shouldn't have done that, you know."

"We need to find a way to catch up," I said.

"I know I'm only here to lend a hand," Ethan said, without

opening his eyes. "But it's not a bad idea. That man can track better than anyone I've ever known."

"Yes, but he has no backup," Vincent said.

"You've rarely worked with a partner, at least until you came here," I said.

"And here I do, so I'd like to keep him alive." Vincent's words had heat behind them. "In case you've forgotten, it was barely a week ago that he was lying in a hospital bed, bleeding to death."

"You're an ass," I said, leaning forward. "I was there, too, but I also know Rider can do this, or have you forgotten that he can sneak up on anyone in the woods? He makes no noise."

"He's not invisible," Vincent said, "and I'm pretty sure the guy we're chasing isn't packing fairy dust and pebbles."

"He'll be careful," I argued.

"Like you are?" Vincent asked.

"What's that supposed to mean?" I yelled.

Vincent's anger erupted and washed over me. My stomach twisted, trying to revolt.

"You know exactly what I mean," Vincent said, his voice growing quiet and cold.

"No," I said, getting to my feet.

Vincent mirrored me and rose to his feet as well.

"No," I repeated, "I don't think I do." Vincent's anger was fueling my own. Inside me, small shards of soul were becoming restless. They started rising and falling in waves, like turbulent seas.

"Did you even-"

"I think everyone needs to settle down," Ethan said, stepping between the two of us.

I saw Vincent's eyes grow black before he looked away. They had been clear while arguing with me, but when he looked at Ethan, they changed. Turning my back to the others,

I took a few meditative breaths. No one could get under my skin like Vincent.

Once I was calmer, I thought it over. With Vincent and Rider being friends, I had been looking at it from Rider's point of view, and at what it meant to him. It obviously meant a lot to Vincent as well.

"I'm sorry I put you in a tight spot," I said, turning back to face him.

"You were right," Vincent said. "We need to find the Lost as quickly as we can."

"Is it always like this?" Ethan asked, arms crossed and leaning against a tree again.

My smile was weak. "Not always."

"Well, we should rest up and not waste energy arguing," Ethan said.

I wanted to give Ethan a quick hug, but it felt awkward to do so with only the three of us there, so I sat back down against my pack again. The sunlight streaked through the trees and I closed my eyes, soaking up its warmth.

Voices woke me up. Rider was back and was talking with Vincent. It was hard to say how much time had passed. The sun was shining, but it looked lower on the horizon than I felt comfortable with. The pressure to move started to take center stage, so I got to my feet and tried to stretch the drowsiness away. How was it possible for me to be more exhausted than I had been before I slept?

"Rider found a way for us to make up some time," Vincent said. "Ready to move?"

Being tired would have to wait. We had a bigfoot to save.

"Ready." My muscles protested the moment I picked up the bag and slung it around to my back. "Can we catch up to them today?"

"I do not think so," Rider said.

"We'll try to get close tonight, but remain far enough back that we can't be seen or heard," Vincent said, as we got moving. "Hopefully, tomorrow we can overtake them."

"What do we do then?" Ethan asked.

My brain must have still been asleep. "What do you mean?"

"You all aren't officially on duty, right?" Ethan asked. "What do we do when we find this guy?"

"We don't have to be on duty to stop him," Vincent said.

"But stop him how? Are you making an arrest?" Ethan asked. "Does this guy know he's hunting a person, and not an animal?"

"He knows what he's hunting." I tried not to sound defensive, but I was surprised by Ethan's remarks.

"If he's a hunter, he's armed," Ethan said. "If you all are arresting him, or them, since I'm still not clear on if we're after one or two people, then we might want to discuss how to go about it."

"It's too early to tell," Vincent said. "We'll have to assume that if he knows he's hunting an intelligent person, he'll have no qualms with shooting us."

My stomach dropped. I hated the idea of being shot at.

"That's what I thought, too," Ethan said.

"But we're at the mercy of the terrain when deciding tactics," Vincent added. "Cass and I have tracked hunters before with Logan. Coming at them from three sides worked well in that situation. It might be our best option here."

"I'm not sure it worked 'well' before," I said under my breath.

A ghost of a grin showed up on Vincent's face, but he didn't respond.

Weariness weighed heavy on everyone. I could see it on their faces. Even Rider was affected by the day's effort. The insistent need to move farther, faster, drove me forward, but my pace grew gradually slower throughout the evening. Well before the sun went down, Vincent called a halt for the day.

"Maybe we should go a little farther," I suggested.

"We could, but the more rest we get today, the better off we'll be tomorrow when we catch up," Vincent said. He came over and helped me out of the backpack when I fumbled with the clasp. "We'll get him."

Nodding, I sank to the ground and dug through my bag. My fatigue was so great that even the rough ground felt comfortable on my aching muscles. Ethan came over and sat next to me. When I leaned into his shoulder, he wrapped an arm around me.

"Today was quite the day," Ethan said. "How are you holding up?"

"Tired," I admitted without thinking, "how about you?

"It's been a while since my military days, but this isn't the first time I've been on my feet all day. From the looks of it, this isn't the first time for your partners, either."

Rider and Vincent were both slowly setting up camp. They appeared to be ignoring us, but I knew they could both hear.

"Maybe," I said. Before we met Rider had spent a lot of time outdoors, I knew that, but little else. Vincent used to track people and creatures, sometimes for days, before taking them between the worlds. He didn't talk about it, but I always pictured him battling the bad guys, disappearing with them, and then leaving them trapped in limbo. Sure, sometimes he took their souls, but I tried not to think about that.

"I'm sorry our vacation got derailed," I said. Seeing the others at work forced me to my feet again.

"Don't be," Ethan said. "I'm with you, and we're helping a bigfoot, of all things. I'm pretty sure there aren't many people who can say they've ever done that."

"Probably not," I admitted.

After setting up camp and eating, Ethan hoisted our packs into the air again to discourage nighttime visitors digging into our food.

"Rider, are you okay for the first watch?" Vincent asked.

"I am," Rider said.

"I'll pick up where he leaves off," Ethan said.

Vincent nodded. "I'll take over and wake everyone early again."

"What about me?" I asked, trying to stifle a yawn.

"Three watches will get us through the night," Vincent said.

I put my hand on my hip and glared. "But with four, everyone gets more sleep."

He looked frustrated, but was clearly too tired to argue. "I'll wake you for your turn."

Sleep came easy. The breeze rocked the hammock slightly and I was dead to the world before the sun went down.

When Vincent woke me, it was still dark and I only had vague recollections of dreams filled with distorted images. Even after the day we had yesterday, I was glad to be awake.

After handing over his gun and making sure I would wake everyone at the first sign of light, Vincent went back to bed, leaving me alone in the dark.

Flashlights would have ruined any night vision, not to mention light us up to anyone nearby, so I leaned against a tree and watched the shadows. What did the guys do when they were on watch? I guess I should have asked, but everyone else seemed instinctively to know what they were supposed to do. There was enough moonlight that I could look for moving shadows. That got old fast. Staring at shadows too long could have you thinking something was moving, even if it wasn't.

Knowing that Vincent was nearly blind in the dark made

me think of listening to the sounds. The trees creaked. The leaves rustled. A twig cracked.

My head jerked in the direction of the sound. There were lots of animals in the woods, right? It could be a rabbit or a raccoon or something. Crackling of leaves sounded behind me, hidden behind the tree. I didn't move. When I heard the noise again, I looked around the tree and saw nothing. Snapping wood and what sounded like footsteps had me whirling around again. When I looked uphill, I saw it.

Outlined in the moonlight was the sleek fur of a large dog. I say dog because my mind couldn't wrap itself around the word wolf. I like to hike, but I'm not what you would call outdoorsy. Wolf, coyote, dog...whatever it was, it was huge. It stood there and watched me.

Animals don't attack people for no reason. Right?

The beast took a step towards me.

Typically, they probably wouldn't attack unless provoked, but this was me.

Crap. I wasn't going to shoot it. It wasn't its fault that it thought of me as a weak link that needed to be killed. Plus, a gunshot wouldn't be the smartest noise to make when tracking a killer. At least, not if we wanted to remain hidden.

It took a few more steps and bared its teeth.

Do I wake the guys or deal with this myself? Could I even make the thing back down now that it had targeted me?

Yesterday had been a long day. The least I could do was try to deal with this on my own.

It loped closer and I kept my eyes on it, while I opened the Path. When I saw the creature's Path, I took a step back and reached automatically for my gun. It was the same Path that we had been following. It was an animal. That was certain, but its Path was complex, like a person's. I had no idea what it meant, but I didn't like it. The animal also wasn't growling. It was baring its teeth and moving towards me, but wasn't making a sound.

Moving slowly to one side, I went to Rider's hammock and without looking away, I shook it. The dog stopped and cocked its head. Rider didn't move. I pushed on the hammock again with no success. Turning around, I pulled the side of the bed back and shook Rider.

His arm shot and slammed into me, shoving me back several paces. He might as well have hit me with a brick. Dropping the gun, I clasped my hands to my chest. Rider twisted and fell out of his bed. When he jumped up, he issued a growl.

"Cass?" Vincent sounded worried, and I heard him get out of bed.

I was me. None of the soul shards had tried to take over so I was completely myself. Rider was my friend and he wouldn't hurt me on purpose, but the adrenaline pumping through my veins told a different story. One that screamed at me to run away. Instead, I pointed to where the animal had been and fell to my knees, trying to get a grip on my breathing and the throbbing pain that radiated outward.

"Cass, what's going on?" Vincent was at my side, putting an arm protectively around me.

Rider walked over, but he wasn't paying attention to the woods, so I pointed again, unable to catch my voice. If it weren't for the fact that Rider looked confused, I might have been worried about his approach.

"Cass, talk to me," Vincent said.

Rider picked me up and set me back down on my feet. I coughed and tried to get more air into my burning lungs. Hunched over, one hand still on my chest, I pointed a shaky finger back into the woods again.

I managed to spit out, "There was a wolf." Saying dog wouldn't have sounded big enough for all this trouble.

Rider looked into the darkness. "There is nothing close to us. I would have smelled an animal."

I coughed again, causing my chest to spasm further. While hugging my chest, I hunched over, wanting to curl up on the ground, but Vincent kept me standing until Rider nudged him out of the way.

Fury and worry exploded out of Vincent, and his voice was ice. "You need to tell me what's going on, right now."

It almost felt like I had been struck again and I stepped away from Vincent. He must have realized why, because he swore under his breath and walked out of sight.

"It's out there," I called after Vincent. Why wouldn't they listen to me?

Rider circled around me before leaning down, nose to nose with me. Rider looked into my eyes. "You are you."

"No shit," I spat. My breathing came easier, but the pain wasn't going anywhere.

"Why shouldn't she be herself?" Ethan asked.

Hearing the irritation in his voice was not helping the situation.

"She is not always herself," Rider said as if it being someone different was an everyday occurrence. To me he said, "Take off your shirt."

"What?" Ethan hissed.

I shook my head and closed my eyes. Could this morning get any worse?

SEVEN

"Everyone stop!" I didn't raise my voice, but the words came out with force. I moved back and leaned against a tree.

"What-"

I interrupted Ethan. "No. Stop. Rider, there was a large animal out there. It's the same one we were tracking."

He frowned and shook his head. "I would have-"

"Well, you didn't," I snapped. "His Path is there."

"It's gone now," Vincent said, stepping back into our campsite. "Whatever it was is gone."

I wanted to scream out in frustration, but knew it would do no good.

"Why don't you tell us what happened." Vincent kept his voice calm.

I rolled my eyes and ignored Rider when he lifted one of my arms to inspect it. "There was a large dog. It looked like a wolf. When I checked its Path, it was the same one we had been following."

Rider let go of that arm and pulled the other away from my chest. I winced, but let him hold the arm out for his inspection.

"Then what happened?" Vincent asked, still in that same calm voice. He had reined in his emotions to the point that his face may as well have been carved in stone.

"I woke up Rider." I stopped, not sure how to continue.

"And?" Ethan asked.

"I struck her," Rider said in the same passive 'it doesn't matter' voice.

That grated on my nerves, but I knew why he sounded that way.

"What?" Ethan's fists clenched.

Vincent closed his eyes.

"We're overlooking the fact that there was an animal out there." I really wanted to derail Ethan from the conversation he was trying to start. "One that was with the hunter."

"So we're supposed to ignore the fact that he hit you?" Ethan was all but trembling from anger.

I shrugged and instantly regretted it as a sharp jolt of pain went through me. "I woke him up out of a dead sleep. He didn't even know it was me."

Rider nodded, but said nothing. Instead, he pulled me gently away from the tree. After he moved my arm back to where it had started, he circled around me again.

"That's what you're going with?" Ethan's frustration accented every word.

"That's what happened," I said, trying to keep my own aggravation in check.

"Rider and I should check the woods," Vincent said in his monotone voice.

"Yes," I responded, feeling some relief. "Go look around. Find whatever animal it was."

"Ethan, you'll look after her?" Vincent waited for a nod from Ethan before turning away.

After making one more pass around me, Rider followed, going in the direction I had indicated. Watching intently, I didn't feel better until they had reached the point where I was sure the wolf had been standing.

"Are you okay?" Ethan asked.

"Um, I think so." I tried to stand up straighter, but grimaced. "I will be, anyway. I'm more worried about what was out there."

"This wasn't what I expected," Ethan said. "I'm not sure what to do here."

"About Rider?" I asked. "Nothing."

"Has anything like this happened before?" Ethan asked.

The image of Rider doped up on meth flashed through my head, but I pushed that thought away. "You mean have I ever tried to shake awake a sleeping werewolf?" I grinned, trying to make light of it. "I think that's a mistake you only make once."

"Let sleeping werewolves lie?" Ethan asked.

"Something like that." I was relieved he was moving away from anger.

"Is there anything I can do for you?" Ethan asked.

Ethan looked like he needed to help me in some way. "I could use some water, but we should also pack up so we can get on the move when they get back."

While Ethan started to take down the camp, I snatched the bottle of pain pills and took a few before making my own attempts at helping, starting with finding Vincent's gun.

The sky was starting to turn light when Rider and Vincent returned.

"Did you find anything?" I asked.

Rider started to take down his hammock, so Vincent answered. "We aren't sure."

"How can you not be sure?" I asked.

"Rider couldn't smell anything, but there were signs something had been there," Vincent said.

"So, there's something out there that looks like a giant wolf, but doesn't have a scent?" I asked, trying to ignore the fact that the animal was becoming larger in my memory.

"We aren't sure," Vincent repeated. I saw his eyes dart to Ethan and back. "Everything good?"

"I think so." I realized that my answer was as vague as Vincent's had been. "We need to get moving, though. Do we have a plan for the day?"

"Get as close as we can, circle around if possible, and close in," Vincent said.

Nodding, I handed over his gun. "You're going to need this."

He hesitated, but took it.

"I think we have everything," Ethan said.

Looking around, I saw that Ethan and Rider had packed up and were ready to move. The hateful backpack was waiting for me, but before I had a chance to grab it, Rider picked it up wordlessly and once again took the lead on our hunt.

With discomfort radiating through my chest, it was such a relief that I didn't have to wear the thing that I didn't even argue. Later in the day, I could always pick it up again.

The pace was quick, but it didn't feel fast enough. Unfortunately, it was all I could do to keep up, and I could tell that Ethan and Vincent were struggling as well. Complaining wouldn't help, so I kept it to myself. When Rider stopped a few hours later, I was grateful for the break, but felt bad since I wasn't carrying anything and was still worn out.

"I can carry my bag now," I lied.

Rider looked around before shaking his head. "I think we should leave the bags here."

That perked me up. "How close are we?"

"We are close enough that I do not think we should make much noise once we leave this location," Rider said.

"This is it then," I said.

Vincent nodded. "It is. When we get close enough, Rider, you signal us and then circle around to one side, and I'll go the other direction. Cass and Ethan will give us twenty minutes and then move forward again."

"We'd cast a wider net if Ethan and I split up as well," I said.

"We don't have enough weapons to go around," Vincent said.

"He doesn't know that. Besides, I have the Path," I said.

He looked like he was thinking it over, but he was almost too animated, which made me wonder if he actually had.

"No," he said after giving it some time. "We don't know what to expect. Three sides will work best."

The argument was on the tip of my tongue when Ethan came up beside me and took my hand.

"I think it's a good plan," Ethan said.

Knowing I was outvoted, and there was no way I was going to win, I agreed. After the bags had been lifted into the trees we continued as quietly as we could after our quarry. We moved faster without our bags holding us down, but it was still over an hour before Rider stopped us and made a bunch of complicated hand gestures.

Ethan and Vincent nodded, so I shrugged in way of agreement, and then Ethan and I were alone. I wanted to pace, but the thought of tripping and making a bunch of noise rooted me to the spot. It might have been comforting to be closer to Ethan, but he looked lost in his own little world. His face was the picture of seriousness.

Time crawled by and I spent it worried the others wouldn't

be in place, or that the hunter would have moved so far ahead that we'd miss him. My stomach tightened like a coiled spring and yet we still stood there waiting.

When Ethan signaled us to move forward, I wanted to run ahead, but I managed to rein myself in and follow Ethan's lead. Telling myself that letting Ethan go first had nothing to do with the fact that, in my compulsive worry, I forgot which direction we were going. There are times when I'm really good at lying to myself.

We started up a hill, which caused even more uncertainty. Even I knew that being downhill from someone shooting at you was an extreme disadvantage. There was no sign of our hunter, though. Ethan held up his hand near the top of the hill, stopping me. He inched himself forward while I stewed in my frustration below the crest of the rise. After surveying the area, Ethan motioned me forward again.

"Put your hands up!" I heard Vincent's yell, but it seemed far away and he wasn't in sight.

Ethan lunged forward and I was fast on his heels. We stopped before a drop-off. Below, Vincent approached a man sitting on the ground with his hands up. Vincent's gun was trained on the stranger and I saw Rider approaching from the opposite side.

The man didn't move. I could hear him talking, but I wasn't close enough to hear to what he was saying. There was no resistance when Rider stood him up and wrapped zip strips around his wrists.

"Huh," Ethan said, holstering his weapon. "That was simple enough." He pulled me into a kiss, which I wasn't expecting, but was pleasantly surprised to receive. "Let's get down there."

We had to walk a short way to find an incline that would

allow us to get down the hill without falling. When we caught up with them, the man was still sitting on the ground, hands bound behind his back, and Vincent stood over him.

"This is an awful lot of trouble to go to for one camper." He smiled as though there was a joke that no one else got.

"This," Vincent said, "is Peter."

"How do you do, Miss," Peter said.

Besides his hands bound behind his back, he looked like any other person enjoying their day. A little dirty, maybe, but I didn't even want to think about how grimy I felt.

"Where's Rider?" I asked.

"He went on ahead to make sure everything is okay," Vincent said. "And Peter was getting ready to tell us what he's doing out here."

"Was I?" Peter asked.

"You were." Vincent's voice was calm and his face remained as impassive as ever, but I could tell this guy was already frustrating him.

"Darling," Peter turned to me, "why is a lovely woman like you out here with these men?"

Feeling creeped out, my nose curled up involuntarily.

"If you're in some kind of trouble," Peter continued, "just say the word and I'll do what I can do to help you."

"Cass, why don't you go catch up to Rider," Vincent said. "Ethan and I will wait here with Peter."

The lines of tension on Vincent's face were clear to me, and I hesitated.

"Ah, Cass. It's nice to put a name to that pretty face of yours," Peter said.

Ew.

"You can find Rider without any trouble, right?" Vincent didn't take his eyes off Peter when he spoke to me.

"Yeah. I'll catch up to him." Turning away, I pulled up the Path and searched for the direction Rider had headed. I had to force myself to walk slowly because Peter made my skin crawl and there was no way I was going to let him know that I was rattled. For once, I was more than happy to take Vincent's suggestion without argument.

"You be careful out there, Cass," Peter called. "You never know what monsters are lurking in the woods."

"Enough," Vincent said.

Pretending not to hear them was the only good response, so I didn't look back. Hearing the man call me Cass really got under my skin, and it was clearly aggravating Vincent. When I was certain I was out of view, I hurried forward. Rider was following the same trail Harry had taken, and they both had a head start on me. Putting ground between Peter and me was a happy bonus.

A breeze stirred the trees, birds chirped, and small animals moved around unseen on the forest floor. Those sounds together started to make me feel better. Sure, I was miles from civilization, but it was peaceful here.

Leaves crunched underfoot and I started to trudge up a hill. Twice, I saw and heard the quick movements of something small in the undergrowth, but each time, I missed what had made the noise.

Maybe after spending so much time together out here, Rider would start to talk to me again. It wasn't like he had ignored me on the trip. There had been no casual conversation, but we had to start somewhere, right?

By the time I reached the top of the hill, I was winded and my chest ached with each expansion of my lungs. The landscape flattened out on top of the hill until it began to slope down towards a grass and wildflower-filled meadow. This made it easier to catch my breath.

Rider was on the other side of the clearing, walking with a very short, very skinny, and yes, a very furry person. It was hard to say how short at this distance, but Rider towered over the person that I assumed was Harry. Smiling, I drove away the flowing river of the Path.

CHAPTER
EIGHT

"You found him," I said as I started down the hill.

I didn't call out because I didn't have to. Even from this distance, Rider heard me. Apparently, Harry heard me as well, because he stopped dead in the field and then crouched down. Slowing my pace, I watched as Harry appeared to blur and then disappear completely. Even though I had no idea what happened, I knew that I was the cause, so I stopped moving. Rider knelt down on the ground and it looked like he was speaking to the invisible Harry. Since I didn't have super hearing I didn't know what he said, but he did gesture in my direction.

Trying to appear as harmless as possible, I gave a little wave and then froze. Rider and Harry weren't alone in the meadow. The large wolf was frozen in the grass, looking ready to pounce.

"Rider." I tried to keep my voice calm and not startle the animal, in case it heard me as well. "Hide Harry."

He looked up at me, confused.

"Don't argue, don't run, but hide him, preferably off the ground. The wolf is back."

Rider glanced around, but I knew from his crouched position that he wouldn't see the wolf. Even standing it was probably far enough away to hide in the grass.

Now, what do I do?

Rider stood and walked back into the woods. There was a small flurry of moving grass that must have been Harry. I watched the movement carefully, trying to catch a glimpse of Harry. When I looked back to the wolf, it was gone.

Stupid rookie mistake. Not seeing the animal anywhere, I bolted down the hill. There was no way to tell if Rider had moved quickly once out of sight, and I had no way of knowing if they were followed.

"I lost sight of it," I yelled.

Tall prairie grass beat at me as I ran. Tiny seeds and dust flew into the air. My chest screamed with each breath, and burrs clutched at my clothes. The grass grew shorter as I approached the trees where Rider had disappeared.

Moving into the shade of the trees, I heard a high-pitched squeal.

My heart leapt into my throat and my mind instinctively jumped into the Path. There was no damming the flow. The full weight and power crashed over me. Ahead, Rider kneeled over something on the ground. I assumed it was Harry, but there was no time to look.

"Where is it?" I yelled.

"I did not see." There was panic in his voice, which was never good.

My feet pounded into the ground in an attempt to close the distance between my friend and me.

Yards away, I saw the shape dart through the trees, running

straight at Rider. Slamming power into the Path, I lashed out at the creature. It was crude and blunt, but I forced a wall of the Path firm and slammed it straight into the wolf, knocking it to the side.

The animal got to its feet as I reached my partner. Rider's hand was wrapped tightly around Harry's arm, which was bleeding profusely.

The wolf was gone again when I looked back up.

"How bad is it?" I asked, trying to spot any movement in the forest.

"It is bad," Rider said. "There was no smell until it struck."

"Are you injured?" I asked, realizing my voice was louder than necessary, but I couldn't seem to modulate it between gasping breaths.

"I am not," Rider said.

That was something working for us. Glimpsing movement at the edge of my vision, I tried to knock the creature off course again, but it was a waste of energy. The wolf was gone before I made contact.

"Take off your belt and tie it tightly around his arm above the wound." I turned in circles while giving instructions. "But don't let go until it's tight. That will slow the bleeding."

The Path stormed around me, but even with all that power, I was having trouble tracking my quarry. Its Path lightened to almost nothing and then burst back to life somewhere unexpected.

"I've got it," Rider said.

"Good. Grab Harry, we're getting out of here," I said.

Rider picked the small man up, but I didn't take my eyes off the woods.

"Walk in front of me, but slowly. I am having a hard time following this thing," I said. It was an understatement. Even worse, my weariness was making itself known.

A growl to the left had me whipping around to shield us on

that side, but once again, there was nothing there. I dropped our buffer before I used any more energy on it.

"Vincent is nearby," Rider said.

"We need to get him and get out of here." There was an edge of desperation in my voice that made Rider move faster.

Movement in front of him grabbed my attention, but once again, I was too late. "Damnit! This thing-"

It crashed into my side, knocking me down. Wrapping the Path around the creature as I fell wasn't something I intended to do, but the trick worked and I managed to shove it away. Too late, I realized that it had my arm in its jaw.

I hit the ground before the wolf smashed into the tree. It cried out. My own pain hadn't registered, but I knew it was coming. The animal turned to me and growled after it hit the ground. The noise was dark and thick, not only heard, but also felt inside. The sun dimmed and shadows stretched out, appearing darker.

The only thing that kept me from running in fear was the fact that I had heard that sound before. Weeks ago, Rider had made the same noise, bringing terror with only his voice.

The wolf turned and I saw its Path begin to fade.

"Cass!"

I heard my name, but didn't look away.

Not this time.

I grabbed the Path and gave it substance. Using one arm, I scrambled to my feet and followed the fading Path. The trees flickered around me, then the forest began to transform. New growth overrode the old. It exploded upwards and died away before being replaced once again.

Awareness of my pain arose and I saw blood running down my arm. I clasped my hand tightly over the wound, and tried to ignore the feeling of blood on my skin and the agony that spread.

With me holding its Path, I forced the animal to slow. Urging more power forward, I made the wolf stop. It growled again, but it didn't have the effect it did before. The woods around us had died away, but the passage of time stopped when the animal did.

It sat down and looked at me warily. Moving slowly wasn't my choice, but at this point, I felt lucky to be standing. When I got near, I fell to my knees and looked directly into the creature's eyes.

It couldn't be a werewolf. Rider would have known if it had been, wouldn't he? Those vivid blue eyes held intelligence, though.

"What are you?" I asked.

It cocked its head and watched me.

"What do I do with you?" I asked. "You walk the Path, but you came out and hurt someone. I don't understand why."

"Cassie?"

I looked around and saw Rider. He approached slowly and squatted down next to me.

"Do you see him?" I asked.

Rider shook his head.

I sighed and closed my eyes, which was a mistake. Vertigo gripped me, and it remained even after I opened my eyes.

"You have gone too far. I am bringing you back," Rider said.

"I don't know what to do with him," I said. Bright white lights began to twinkle before bursting. I closed my eyes to shield them, but that was a mistake. It was difficult to open them again.

"We will figure that out at another time. Are you ready?" Rider asked.

A free feeling started to fill me, and I nodded, dazed.

I looked at the wolf. "You, stay."

Rider's arms folded around me. I heard the creature bark, and then I closed my eyes.

It felt like my body slammed into a brick wall before being ripped back and slammed into another. The Path fell away and my stomach heaved. I pushed away from Rider before losing my stomach contents.

Voices and noise came from what seemed a long way off. I felt disconnected from the sound. The ground felt soft under me, so I rolled away from my own mess and stared up, watching the sunlight flash through the leaves on the tree.

Someone pushed down on my arm, but the pain wasn't as bad as it had been before. Turning, I saw Vincent. Although he tried to hold his mask of indifference, I saw through it and recognized the severe look he wore underneath.

He was talking, but I couldn't make it out. Somehow, I thought I should be able to understand, but it didn't seem important. My good arm wobbled when I reached up, and with a finger, I traced the small scar that slashed Vincent's temple. I smiled at him before letting my arm fall.

I never did ask him how he got that scar.

Feeling more tired than I think I had ever felt before, I closed my eyes. Something stung my face. My eyes popped open and I glared at Vincent.

His eyes were flat black, but he put his hand lightly against the cheek that stung.

Something had gone wrong when I came back. The world had sounded distant, but now silence was settling in. Vincent was still talking, and I looked around to see who he was speaking to. A short, naked, hairy man stood on my other side. Behind him, I saw Rider, eyes closed, leaning against a tree.

A whining noise broke the silence. Turning my head to look behind Vincent, I saw the wolf. Its head was cocked and it watched me as though trying to figure out what I was.

"I thought I told you to stay." I'm not sure if I said it out loud or in my head. Looking around, I couldn't tell if anyone else saw the animal.

I took a deep breath and felt like I was floating. I stared at the sky again, seeing if I was getting any closer to the treetops. Vincent's face once again blocked my view, but I saw that his eyes were back to normal and I could pick out the golden flecks that gleamed out of the green. He looked sad, but calmer as well, which was good.

My eyelids were growing heavy and the need for sleep couldn't be denied any longer. With my good hand, I sought out Vincent's and gripped it before I closed my eyes.

Maybe if I held on he wouldn't be so worried.

CHAPTER

NINE

"You went about things all wrong today, you know."

Opening my eyes, I saw that I was still in the forest. It was dark, but there was a fire nearby. Vincent sat beside me, still holding my good hand. Seeking out the voice, I saw an old man seated on a nearby rock smoking a pipe. The wolf sat by his side while the old man scratched its ears.

"You're that old coot I saw in the woods weeks ago." My muscles felt like water, but feeling prone on the ground, I reluctantly extracted my hand from Vincent's and pushed myself up to a sitting position. No one else in the camp moved.

"Is that what you call me or your grandmother?"

I frowned. "Both. I told you that before."

The old man grumbled under his breath and smoked his pipe. Vincent didn't acknowledge our discussion, which told me I must have been dreaming. Gran said entering dreams was a trick this man knew well.

"Is that wolf yours?" I asked. "It nearly killed people, one of them being me."

The old man patted the creature's head. "Good wolf."

"Good wolf? Did you send it out here?"

The old man cackled until he started coughing. I crossed my arms and waited until he got control of himself again.

"You cannot own a person," he said. "Many have tried in the past, but the spirit is hard to break."

"The wolf attacked us on its own, then?" I asked.

"No, no, no. You jump and run around, but you do not think. I'm not convinced that you are the you we need."

"I'm the only me there is. If you're going to be rude, you can go away. I've had a long day and I need to sleep."

"Okay. Yes, yes. You are you." The old man muttered and bobbed his head as though talking to someone else.

"I'm going back to sleep." I adjusted my sleeping bag, stalling to see if he would say anything else.

"You are like your grandmother." It almost sounded like a begrudging compliment.

"She talked about you a little when I told her you said hello," I said.

He sat up a bit straighter. "What did she say?"

"Nope. I'm not saying anything until you tell me what's going on," I said.

"What's going on? What's going on?" He slid off his rock and started to pace. "Everywhere there are things going on."

I crossed my arms again. "Fine, what's going on out here? Why did it," I pointed at the wolf, which hadn't moved, "attack Harry? And me?"

"That? That's what you want to know? Out of everything, everywhere, that's what you want to find out?" He seemed confused and disappointed.

"Right now, yes. I nearly died because of it."

"That was your own recklessness. You cannot blame the wolf for that."

I sighed. "Either give me answers or go away."

"You see this wolf standing here?"

"Of course I can," I said.

"Your friends did not see him. They did not even believe he existed until it was too late."

"They believed me," I said, not feeling confident in the statement, "and Rider saw him when he attacked."

He shrugged, which was an odd movement for the man. His back seemed to puff out and move independently under his clothes.

I shifted uncomfortably, wondering why I was still talking with this madman.

"How lonely is a life when it is lived alone?" he asked. "No one sees you, hears you, or talks to you. There is no one to look in your direction, even if you follow them around. What would a person like that do when it met someone who acknowledged their existence?"

I looked at the wolf. To live surrounded by people and never be seen? Lonely seemed too weak of a word.

"That person," he continued, "the one person who sees you, would you believe what that person says? Would you do what that person asked?"

"Peter saw him," I said.

"The man used the wolf as a hunting dog."

"That's awful." I looked at the wolf, unsure of which side the creature might be on. "Is he...still friends with Peter?"

"He is not."

"Oh," I responded, unsure of what else to say.

"I gave you your answers and now you give me mine." He was practically bouncing in his eagerness.

"About Gran? She said you two used to see each other." It sounded lame after what the man had told me, so I wracked my brain for something nice. "I asked her if she wanted to see you again. I offered to take her to the woods where I met you."

"And?"

"And...she didn't say no. She told me she would let me know."

The man appeared to turn his mind inward, and I thought I could see a smile under the beard, but it was hard to tell.

I watched the wolf, giving the man a moment. It cocked its head again, so I held out my good hand to let him sniff me if he wanted.

"Do you have a name?" I asked.

"He has had many names," the old man said.

"But what does he like to be called?"

"He would answer to Fenrir, despite what I told him about what humans think of the name. He is looking for his family or their descendants."

"Hello, Fenrir," I said.

The wolf barked a high-pitched yap, which sounded neither upset nor happy.

He only stared at my hand, so I dropped it and turned my attention back to the old man.

"Why are you and your friend so interested in me?" I asked.

"Fenrir?" he asked.

"The other old man. He...I don't know, stopped time or something."

The muttering started again. I heard the words 'show off,' and grinned.

"Well?" I asked.

"Ask him, if you are so friendly with him."

I rolled my eyes and crossed my arms, waiting for a response.

"I am not yet convinced that you are the you we are looking for," he said.

"That's getting old." I looked back at the wolf, who was watching us both. "Are you friends with that old coot?" I asked the wolf.

"Fenrir is being much more cautious with choosing his friends," the man said.

"Good for you," I said. "As you long as you don't try to kill us, stop by and visit if you want. Now, if you'll both excuse me, I'm exhausted."

"You are no use to anyone if you kill yourself," the old man said as I laid down.

I swept my hand at him in a go-away fashion, got comfortable, and then I looked around the camp. It must be Vincent's turn on watch. He was the only one around the fire. Carefully, I slipped my hand back into his and closed my eyes. Before I drifted off to sleep, or maybe I was waking up, I gently squeezed his hand.

"Cass?" Vincent murmured.

If it had been anyone else, I probably would have kept my eyes shut. However, I remembered the look on his face when Rider brought me back.

"I'm up." My muscles felt even more useless than they had before.

He didn't say anything, but his hand twitched in mine. Afraid he was going to pull it away, I held on tighter. Awareness started to steal over me.

"Is everyone okay?" I asked.

Vincent shook his head and my heartbeat ramped up a few notches.

"Rider?" I asked. I let go of Vincent and tried to push myself up to a sitting position. Pain convulsed through me and my bad arm collapsed. "Harry? Was Harry okay? Where's Ethan?"

"Lay down before you hurt yourself," Vincent said. "They're fine. Mostly, anyway."

I tried to use only my good arm to push myself up.

"Don't," Vincent said. "They're all right."

"You said-"

"It's okay," he said. "Ethan's asleep. Harry's injured, but he'll recover. Once Harry determined you would be fine, Rider left."

"Left? What do you mean left?" I asked.

"I mean, he walked into the woods and no one has seen him for hours," Vincent said.

"We should go after him." Thinking about how lonely the wolf was, I thought I might tear up. "He shouldn't be alone out there."

"I think he needs some time to himself," Vincent said.

That hurt, but I knew Vincent was right. Rider was okay, and that was the important thing.

"Were you hurt?" I asked.

The only response I received was silence.

"Vincent?"

"No injuries."

"That doesn't sound convincing."

"It was a long day," Vincent said.

"Too long," I agreed.

"You disappeared."

My mind didn't follow the shift in conversation, so I hazarded a guess. "When I followed after Rider?"

"No, when I met the two of you in the woods."

I tried to replay the scene in my head, but some things were still jumbled together. "I don't think I saw you."

"You were bleeding. You walked into the woods and then you were gone."

I tried to think back, but gave up.

"Rider said this wasn't the first time you disappeared," Vincent said.

"It wasn't. At least, that's the way Logan described it." The fact that everyone was okay started to sink in. That small stress had taken too much effort and with its release, I felt drained.

"No one told me," Vincent said.

It was true. It happened after Vincent had left without a word, and things had been busy since he returned, but this definitely wasn't the time to bring that up.

"Sorry," I said.

"You're here now, though."

"You don't sound too thrilled about that," I said.

"You may have some trouble with Ethan," Vincent said.

"What? Why?"

"It...He didn't take it well when I left him behind with Peter."

"Oh, I'm sure that'll be-"

"He also didn't respond well when Rider told him why I knew something was wrong. He didn't know that I was the one that took-"

"It's fine," I said. Vincent taking my soul seemed like it had happened a lifetime ago.

Vincent shook his head.

"It's fine," I said again. "I'll talk with Ethan. If I'm not upset about it, he shouldn't be."

"He's probably more concerned than anything," Vincent said.

"He already knew about my soul."

"Concerned about you and me."

"Oh." I sighed. That wasn't going to be a fun conversation. "Once I explain, I'm sure he'll drop it."

"Maybe he shouldn't," Vincent said.

"Why not?"

The crackling fire was my only response.

"Vincent?" I asked.

"Sorry," he said. "It's been a long day."

"I'll talk to him," I said again. "I'm sure he won't mind being woken up."

Vincent nodded. "I know he won't. You should get some rest first."

Even our short conversation had worn me out, so I didn't argue and settled back down in my sleeping bag.

"If you see the wolf, don't hurt it," I said.

Vincent didn't say anything.

"I mean it." It would have sounded better if I hadn't yawned immediately after saying the words. "Let the others know too."

"Why should we do that?" Vincent asked.

"It's..." I tried to put words to what my heart was feeling. "It was used. Tricked by Peter." I yawned again.

"Get some rest."

"Promise me?"

Vincent sighed. "You'll fill me in later?"

Even through the pain and exhaustion, I felt relief. "Of course."

When I woke up next, I stared up at the stars and Ethan was next to me. Reaching out, I took his hand and he nearly jumped.

"Hey," I said through bleary eyes.

"Morning," he said.

"Is it morning already?"

"Not morning enough for light, but morning all the same."

"The stars are out."

"This isn't really how I pictured us watching them," Ethan said. He sounded tired, but I could tell he was uncomfortable talking to me as well.

Since I had no idea how to drag out what Ethan was think-ing, I laid there and let him come around to it in his own time.

"How are you feeling?" Ethan asked.

"Exhausted, but my arm doesn't hurt as bad," I said.

"They said Harry fixed you up. Who knew a bigfoot would have so much medical skill?"

I bristled at the implication that Harry should somehow be less capable, but thought the better of saying anything at the moment. "Whatever he did worked. Did you meet him?"

"Yeah, Rider introduced us after Harry finished with your arm."

"How was Rider? I only caught a glimpse of him-"

"Why didn't you tell me?" Ethan asked.

I guess he was ready to talk about it. "Tell you what?"

CHAPTER

TEN

Ethan let out a short, frustrated sigh, but looked like he was trying to keep most of his agitation reined in. "About you and Vincent."

"I've told you before that nothing is going on between Vincent and me."

He wouldn't look at me. "I don't pretend to know. I mean, really know what a person's soul is, or what it looks like. But sharing one with someone, with another man, then that sounds like there's something between you."

"I can't help what it sounds like. It was a side effect of what happened." That it was a side effect of Vincent taking my soul and giving it back was the last thing I wanted Ethan to be thinking about, so I didn't say the words.

"A side effect. Huh." He looked down and seemed like he was trying hard not to be upset. Even with the Path closed, I could tell it wasn't working well. "Then, what's the side effect of him having a piece of you inside of him?"

There was no way I was telling Ethan how deeply Vincent

knew me from taking my soul. For a short time, I was a part of him and now Vincent probably knew more about my past than I knew myself.

"He senses things." It was a vast understatement, but it was a lie I could live with.

Ethan shook his head. "I feel like I've stepped into a place that I shouldn't be."

"You've stepped into my world," I said, trying to lighten the mood a little. "That's all."

"You and I haven't been seeing each other that long. Since I met you, I've seen things and done things beyond my wildest imagination."

"Like protecting Harry?"

A ghost of a smile came across his face, but only lasted moments. "Meeting a bigfoot was a big one. I've seen a lot and I've rolled with the punches as best I could."

"You faced the fairy."

We both grinned at the memory and Ethan looked at me again.

"I think facing your rabbit was a bigger feat," Ethan said.

"Poor Frank," I said, thinking of my dead, but still hopping rabbit.

"But you and Vincent? I'm not sure that-"

"Vincent has made it very clear to me, to everyone, that he wants to fix what he broke and nothing else."

Ethan shook his head. "You didn't see him before he ran off to find you. When he knew something had gone wrong."

Using my good arm, I pushed myself up to a sitting position as best I could. How could I still be so tired after sleeping for so long?

"Lie down," Ethan said.

I raised an eyebrow at him.

Ethan sighed. "Lie down, please?"

"Join me?" I asked.

He looked uncertain at first, but at last, he smiled. "Sure."

Once he had settled in next to me, I put my head at the crook of his neck, ignoring the searing pain across my chest.

I decided honesty was a good way to go here. "I don't know how to fix this."

"I'm not sure it can be," Ethan said.

"Is it something that needs to happen now?" I asked.

"What do you mean?"

"This. This conversation. Does it need to happen now?"

Ethan was quiet for a few moments. "No. I know you're tired. I'm not sure what happened, but I saw you after."

"And in case either of us forgot, we still have almost a week of vacation."

"I assumed you'd want to go with your partners."

"You assumed wrong." I looked up at him to make sure he saw my grin.

"You want to continue our vacation?"

"Well, first I want a bath or maybe two, but yes, I'd like to enjoy the rest of my trip with you."

Ethan hugged me to him and kissed my forehead, only stopping when I winced at the pain in my chest.

"Sorry," he said.

"It's okay."

"Are you all right, though?" he asked. He pulled his arm out from under me and propped himself up.

"I am," I said.

His response was to look me over more carefully. Then he brushed his hand down the side of my face.

We smiled at each other. Not quite sad, but not exactly cheerful either.

Noise in the woods made Ethan look up. Despite my pain and fatigue, I looked over as well.

"It's the wolf," I said.

Ethan was off the ground before I knew it.

"No, don't scare him," I said. Leveraging myself up was difficult. Everything hurt.

"Where is it?" Ethan hissed.

Seeing the gun in his hands, I strained to get to my feet as quickly as I could. I held Ethan's arm to keep myself up. He tried to put himself between the woods and me, but I wouldn't let him.

"It's okay," I said, trying to stay calm while I pushed his gun to the ground. "He's not going to hurt us." Then I heard the animal growl. "At least I don't think..."

The wolf wasn't looking at us. He was looking towards a tree quite a bit away from where we camped.

"What's he watching?" I took a step towards him and Ethan gripped my arm.

"What are you doing?" Ethan hissed.

"What's over there?" I asked, indicating the tree. "Is Rider back?"

"That's where Peter is," Ethan said.

"Oh no," I muttered. "Not good."

My heart beat faster. I tried to lurch away from Ethan, but he still held my arm tightly.

"Are you crazy?" he asked. "Where is it?"

I could hear Peter's voice in the distance.

"We have a man in custody," I whispered an explanation as fast as I could, "and he's about to get murdered on our watch."

If there's one thing that Ethan always understood, it's that work is work.

"Stay next to me," Ethan muttered.

At least he was going in the right direction. When I moved faster, he kept pace.

I heard the wolf growl and Peter started talking rapidly.

"Fenrir," I called.

The wolf looked at me, his teeth bared.

"Wait. Please, you can't do this."

Fenrir didn't move when I put myself between him and Peter. Extracting my arm from Ethan's hand, I knelt down in front of Fenrir. He licked his lips, but his teeth were no longer bared.

"Ethan, can you take Peter back to the camp?" I asked.

Peter made a noise that almost sounded like a return growl. "That mutt can-"

"You," I whipped my head around and glared at Peter, as Fenrir growled, "can shut up and be thankful I'm not feeding you to him." It was harsh, but the man deserved harshness for the way he had treated the wolf.

Still, there was a way to do things and letting Fenrir kill him wasn't the way.

"Is the wolf here?" Ethan asked.

"Yes, please, move Peter away," I said again, turning my attention to the white wolf in front of me.

"I can't leave you here alone-"

"I'm here," Vincent said, walking out of the shadows.

Ethan let out a frustrated breath.

"I'll take Peter," Vincent said.

"No," Ethan said. "If something happens, I think you'll be of more use here than I would." He didn't sound happy about it, but he untied Peter and took him away.

Fenrir growled louder when Peter moved.

"Wait," I said when the wolf stepped forward towards Ethan's retreat. "I know you're angry, and you have every right to be, but do you really want to kill him?"

Fenrir looked at me grimly, and I could feel the fire from his gaze.

"We're not helping him," I said, trying to reassure him. "I know it must look like that, but he's going to pay for what he did out here. He'll be locked up."

Fenrir licked his lips again and sat down, but he looked reluctant.

I moved off my knees and sat in a more comfortable position.

"You don't have to hurt him to get back at him."

Fenrir bared his teeth for a moment.

"Yeah, I'd like to at least kick Peter in the jewels and watch him flail around for a while-"

Vincent chuckled behind me, but I ignored him.

"-but I won't. He's tied up, and we're taking him to where he can't hurt anyone anymore."

Fenrir gave an angry grunt, but I'm pretty sure he understood. He might even have agreed with me, but it was hard to tell.

We stared at each other for a while, and I held my hand out again.

"Cass." The warning in Vincent's voice was clear.

Fenrir had moved forward, but stopped when Vincent's spoke.

Glancing back, I saw Vincent move to stand beside me.

My mind was starting to feel fuzzy, so I didn't discount his worry. "Do you see him?" I asked.

"No," Vincent said.

"Then shush," I said with a smile and turned back to Fenrir. "It's okay."

He didn't move, and I let my hand drop.

"I understand," I said. "You don't have to come any closer." I yawned and started to blink heavily. The shadows around us were condensing and falling away as the sky began to lighten.

Fenrir shook himself from head to tail. He looked almost as tired as I felt. He turned and trotted off a few paces.

"I'm not sure where you live or how you get around, but you can visit," I said.

He looked back in acknowledgment, then walked a few paces and vanished.

"I think he'll leave Peter alone," I said. "Not that Peter deserves it."

"Is he gone?" Vincent asked.

"Yeah."

Vincent squatted down next to me. "You okay?"

"I must look really crazy talking with the air, huh?" I grinned and wavered.

"You look tired," Vincent said.

I stretched, but winced and drew back in on myself. "I'm not sure I've ever been this tired."

Vincent motioned behind him back to camp. "Everything else okay?"

What was there to say to that? "I don't know." It was the best answer I could give. "For now, maybe?"

"Think you can make it back on your own steam?"

My nose scrunched up automatically. I hated being carried.

"I'd prefer to at least try," I said.

"Wait here and let me get Ethan," Vincent said.

The confusion must have been written across my face.

"I don't want to make things more complicated," Vincent explained. "Take it from me, it's better this way."

The thought made me sad, and the realization that Vincent was trying to tread so carefully took me by surprise. "You've seemed different on this trip. Lighter, almost."

Vincent looked confused, and I wasn't sure why I even said it. What I did know was that I needed sleep.

"Don't let this stuff with Ethan and me weigh you down," I said.

"You got it," he said. "You're sure the wolf is on our side?"

"I'm sure he won't hurt us unless provoked."

"Well, don't provoke it. I'll get Ethan."

I pulled my knees into my chest and despite the ache, put my head on my knees and watched Vincent walk away.

When Ethan came to help me, he didn't look as upset as I thought he would be. He helped me to my feet. When I swayed too many times, he picked me up and carried me the rest of the way. It was the last thing I remembered of that night. I must have fallen asleep before we got back.

IT WAS ALMOST noon when I woke up to the quiet camp. No one looked like they were in a hurry.

It didn't take me long to get back on my feet. Sort of, anyway. We debated leaving the site, or staying and waiting for Rider. In the end, we decided that we were running low on food and water, so it was time to go back.

The walk back took a day and a half longer than our trip into the forest, and it was exhausting. Peter soon realized his 'friend' wasn't going to help him out and he turned pretty nasty. When he spoke to me, it was either condescending or lewd, which pissed everyone off, especially me, so I walked well ahead or behind and out of his sight whenever I could.

Harry showed up twice on our way back, but only when Peter was out of sight. Harry examined my arm both times, and each time, he unwrapped it and it looked better. Whatever he was putting on the wound was helping it heal faster than I had anticipated. The last time he visited, his injury had already healed, and he left me an earthen bottle full of a sappy substance and told me to add it to my arm for three more days.

Then he was gone. We avoided his house on our way back, despite the fact that I really wanted to talk with him more, but there was no way we wanted Peter near him.

My daydreams were visions of a shower and a bed, but that vanished when we reached the vehicles. Rider was leaning against his truck, arms crossed, waiting for us.

CHAPTER

ELEVEN

Once I saw him, my heart felt lighter than it had in days. "You're here." I wanted to run up and hug him, but I wasn't sure where we stood.

Ethan went straight up to my friend and shook his hand. "Thank you for what you did. I don't know what it was, but from what little I understand, Cassie wouldn't be here if it weren't for you."

Rider returned the handshake, but only nodded to Ethan, which was then followed by awkward silence.

"Well," Ethan said, "I'll take our bags and give you two a minute." He took my almost-empty backpack and went to his car, leaving Rider and me alone.

It might have been easier if Vincent was there, but he had lagged behind with Peter.

"Are you okay?" I asked.

He nodded.

I stared at him, waiting for more, but I didn't get another reply.

"Are you sure?" I asked. "I've been really worried. We all have."

"There are no lasting side effects from finding you in the Path," Rider said.

"That doesn't really answer the question."

"It was...I was uncertain that you would return."

"But I did," I said with a grateful smile. "Thank you for helping me."

Rider nodded again.

"You've been gone for a few days," I said, not making it a question, but wanting an answer all the same.

"Are you well?" Rider asked.

Would he tell me anything if I asked him directly? Probably not.

"I will be after a shower and sleep," I said.

He wrinkled his nose and stepped away from the truck over to me. He lifted my injured arm carefully and started inspecting it, moving himself around more than jostling my arm.

"Why do you do that?" Ethan came over and joined us.

Rider looked confused but didn't stop. "Because she is injured. If I move her arm more, it could cause more damage. Humans are...fragile."

I'm pretty sure that wasn't what Ethan was asking, but I was more focused on what he said. Hating to be referred to as fragile, I shot Rider a dirty look, which he ignored. He tried to pull up my shirt and I slapped his hand away. He sighed and rolled his eyes.

Rolling his eyes was the one thing I really wished he hadn't picked up from me.

"The wolf did not trouble you?" Rider appeared uncomfortable with the thought as he made a final pass around me.

"No, but we might see him around more," I said.

Rider stood up straight, looking around. "Why should we see the animal again?"

"I don't think he's an animal," I said. "He's a person. I believe he was a very lonely person and paid attention to the first human who saw him and spoke with him. He needed someone as a friend, and he ended up with Peter, who used him."

"That is not a friend," Rider said.

"It's not," I agreed.

"He will be happier if he is friends with us," Rider said.

"I think he will be, yeah." I looked at Rider who was still scanning the woods. "Are you happier-"

"Why did Peter see the wolf?" Rider asked.

I looked away. Rider still wasn't going to talk to me, but I would get it out of him eventually. Right now, though, he only aggravated me.

"I don't know," I said, looking back to see if Vincent had caught up. "I didn't talk to him."

"But you-"

"If you want to know, you can speak to him," I said. "Ethan, I'll help with the packs."

"Okay," Rider said to my retreating back.

Ethan stayed behind for a few seconds, and I heard him say something to Rider, but he caught up to me at his car.

"The packs are taken care of," he said.

I shrugged and started rummaging around in the one I had been using. As an excuse to look busy, I took two pain relievers out of the bottle Vincent and I had passed around the past few days and stowed them in my pocket.

Vincent was in view now, but I waited until he inspected the back seat in Rider's truck and secured Peter inside before I joined them.

"What's going to happen to him?" Ethan asked, gesturing to Peter.

"We still need to talk to Logan, but there's an AIR substation a few hours away," Vincent said, while keeping his face impassive. "That gives Harry a chance to move on before we talk to them."

"Move on? He still has to leave his home?" I remembered all those books that had littered the floor and the beautiful carvings out in the hall. It seemed wrong that Harry needed to move.

"He doesn't have to," Vincent said. "He's choosing to."

It didn't sit well with me, but I nodded.

"I know this wasn't how you planned to spend your vacation, but thanks for the help." Vincent held out his hand to shake Ethan's.

When Ethan didn't hesitate to shake, I had hope that things might be okay between us.

"Enjoy the rest of your vacation. We'll see you when you get back," Vincent said.

Wordlessly, I handed him the bottle I had been holding.

"Thanks," he said.

"Sure, see you around," I said.

Ethan and I walked back to his car. There was a quick conversation taking place behind us, and I turned to look at my two partners.

"Everything okay?" I asked them.

"Yes," Vincent said. "Drive safe."

When Ethan and I left, Vincent and Rider were getting ready to go as well. After leaving them behind, Ethan drove in silence while I watched the trees as we zipped by. We were hours away from the cabin we rented, but I think that was the direction we were heading.

"There's a town up ahead," Ethan said, breaking the long

silence.

Glancing around, I saw the town nestled in a valley between two mountains. Lights were coming on as the shadow of the mountain stretched over.

"It'll be good to get back to some sort of civilization," I said.

"You were injured pretty badly out there. Do you want to see a doctor?" Ethan asked.

"No, Harry did an excellent job on my arm. I might ask Taylor to take a look at it when I get back home, but I don't need to see anyone now."

Ethan nodded and didn't argue. "Do you want to stop here tonight?"

What I really wanted was to get back to our cabin oasis, away from everyone.

The fact that we smelled wasn't lost on me. "It would be nice to get clean and eat real food."

"Real food?" Ethan asked.

"Yes, nothing that is freeze-dried, dehydrated, or in bar form."

"I think we can manage that."

Ethan stopped for gas and came back out with a bag of stuff and directions to a hotel that ended up being not too bad. He ordered food while I locked myself in the bathroom and took stock of my cuts and bruises. I was prepared for the one on my chest, although it looked harsh. The cuts and scrapes over my arms and legs, ones that I hadn't noticed while trekking through the woods, started to burn after I washed.

It probably didn't help that I took the equivalent of two showers, making sure to scrub from head to toe and repeating it in case I missed anything. Getting into clean clothes was divine.

Ethan followed suit, but didn't take nearly as long. The food arrived right before he finished. We talked that evening, avoiding all topics of a serious nature and curled up together that night.

The next day was a little easier. We made it back to the cabin and spent the next few days together. By the second day, we had settled back in and were once again comfortable with each other. We even managed to get out to the ridge one morning to see the stars.

We did exactly what we had planned. We enjoyed the rest of our vacation. I'm not sure how Ethan felt, but on the drive home, it seemed like he was starting to distance himself.

On the other hand, maybe I was.

We agreed to take a few days to catch up on things before we'd call each other.

For me, it was time to face pending psych reviews and trying to get my agent status back to active. The time to run away was over.

Want to read further?
Fractured Worlds (AIR Series Book 6)

WRITING the AIR series has been a fun and amazing experience. There's more planned for Cassie and her partners!

IF YOU ENJOYED THIS BOOK, please leave a review on the site where you made the purchase. Leaving a review helps the reader and author in many ways. Your support is appreciated!

Thank you for reading!

Amanda Booloodian

COMPLETE WORKS

Complete works by Amanda Booloodian:

AIR Series (In Reading Order)
Stonecoat: Novella 0 (AIR Series Book 0)
Shattered Soul (AIR Series Book 1)
Redcap (AIR Series Book 2)
Broken Paths (AIR Series Book 3)
Stolen Sight (AIR Series Book 4)
Fenrisúlfr: Novella 3.5 (AIR Series 5)
Fractured Worlds (AIR Series Book 6)
Reliquary (AIR Series Book 7)
Never-Ending Nightmare (AIR Series Book 8)
Krampus (AIR Series Book 9)
Eclipsed Pathways (AIR Series Book 10)
Void (AIR Series Book 11)
Marked Soul (AIR Series Book 12)

COMPLETE WORKS

AIR Series Box Set
AIR Series Books 0-4: Welcome to the Farm
AIR Series Books 5-8: Conspiracy Theory
AIR Series Books 9-12: Redacted

Spellbound Murder Series
Oath Bound (Spellbound Murder Series Book 1)
Grim Magic (Spellbound Murder Series Book 2)
Fallen Witch (Spellbound Murder Book 3)

Spellbound Murder Box Set
Spellbound Murder Complete Trilogy

AIR Series Audiobooks
Stonecoat: Novella 0.5 (AIR Series Book 0)
Shattered Soul (AIR Series Book 1)
Redcap (AIR Series Book 2)
Broken Paths (AIR Series Book 3)
Stolen Sight (AIR Series Book 4)
Fenrisúlfr: Novella 3.5 (AIR Series 5)
Fractured Worlds (AIR Series Book 6)
Reliquary (AIR Series Book 7)
Never-Ending Nightmare (AIR Series Book 8)
Krampus (AIR Series Book 9)
Eclipsed Pathways (AIR Series Book 10)
Void (AIR Series Book 11)
Marked Soul (AIR Series Book 12)

Spellbound Murder Series Audiobooks
Oath Bound (Spellbound Murder Series Book 1)
Grim Magic (Spellbound Murder Series Book 2)
Fallen Witch (Spellbound Murder Book 3)

ACKNOWLEDGMENTS

In the past few years I've soaked up a lot of knowledge about writing and publishing from countless different places. I'd like to take a moment to acknowledge all the writers who share their knowledge. I've read hundreds of blogs, and probably that amount again in books and articles. Social media conversations have been fun and informative on many levels as well. Thank you all for engaging in the writing community.

A special thank you to JD Book Services and Frankie Sutton, my editors, for all of their assistance and to Deranged Doctor Design who has once again provided me with a wonderful cover and formatting.

Thanks to everyone who made this possible.

ABOUT THE AUTHOR

Amanda Booloodian lives in Missouri with her loving, and often times peculiar, husband. She has been passionate about the written word throughout her life. Now, much of her spare time is spent at the computer, delving into worlds accessible only through vivid imagination. In warm weather, when she isn't pounding on the keyboard, she can often be found wandering through the wilderness. Occasionally she gets it into her head to SCUBA dive or to sit back at home and make wine, which can have interesting results and inspire her writing.

You can find out more about Amanda and her writing, including upcoming releases, on www.Booloodian.com. You can also find her on Facebook: Amanda Booloodian - Author and Instagram: AJBooloodian.